MAT'TA

By
Connie Hartzler

Connie Hartzler / Mat'ta

Table of Contents

Dedication	3
Acknowledgements	4
Foreword and Love Letter from God	5
Chapter One The Wilderness	8
Chapter Two Awakening	36
Chapter Three Braveheart	44
Chapter Four The Shifting	54
Chapter Five Run Home, Mat'ta	63
Chapter Six The Garden	75
Chapter Seven New Beginnings	92
Chapter Eight The Shoreline	124
Chapter Nine The Cross	146
Chapter Ten Preparation	151
About the Author	158

Dedication Page

To the Holy Spirit, who patiently walked me through my wilderness, out of the dark night of my soul, and into abundant joy.

Acknowledgement Page

Michele Kemberling: Papa's gift of living joy in my life, not just the emotion of happiness. Thank you for your inspirational artwork for the Mat'ta series.

Nancy Long: my sister from another mother. Thank you for listening to the reading of Mat'ta as the skeleton took on flesh and became animated by the Holy Spirit. Your measure of faith sustained me when I had little faith of my own.

Gary Hartzler: my husband, my loving Noel. The truth about your character and commitment to Christ are suspended in the allegorical storytelling of Mat'ta. You are my living example of the immense power found only in meekness.

Kim Crinklaw: my sister and friend. Thank you for living the healing, staying in the moment with me, and helping me walk out the truth of the revelations He gave us along the way.

FOREWORD

If you have ever been on a journey with God, and you didn't think you would ever make it out of the wilderness season, this book will help you. It will show you the hidden 'whys' that put you there and it shows you how to get out. This book reminds me of The Shack. It is well written in a story-form like that.

Although you will see her struggle and victory on a deep, personal level, you will also see yourself. Our battles are not the same, but battles are battles, the dark nights of the soul are sure to come should you ever cry out for more of God. He is holy and our carnal nature feels right and safe, but it is not what God wants. God wants us to trust only Him, not ourselves, and to trust Him completely, you will learn to rely on Him the most during the sorrowful times. He is closest to the brokenhearted.

The morning I agreed to help Connie put her precious book in a book format so you can read it, I had only read the first two chapters. I had no idea what the rest of the story would be like, I only knew it was breathed on by God and had to be available to you. I had no idea this was a message to me on a depth that left me in amazement.

The morning I was to start this book, I had a vision and I shook it off and didn't receive it. That morning God said there was an infection in the root. He told me to study roots. I studied taproots and fibrous roots, with no idea she would talk about an infection in the root and the taproot. I have written 10 volumes of *Love Letters from God's Heart to Yours* devotionals and that very morning, God said, read volume 8. I will share below, because it is the love letter from God for you and this book.

May God do His good and perfect work in us, and help us to be all He created us to be and live in a fullness of joy and peace which is by His design. Take the journey to get there, it will be worth it.

Theresa J. Nichols
Author: *Love Letters from God's Heart to Yours*

Psalm 3:1-5 (AMP)

A Psalm of David. When he fled from Absalom his son.
¹ Lord, how they are increased who trouble me! Many are they who rise up against me. ² Many are saying of me, There is no help for him in God. *Selah* [pause, and calmly think of that]! ³ But You, O Lord, are a shield for me, my glory, and the lifter of my head. ⁴ With my voice I cry to the Lord, and He hears and answers me out of His holy hill. *Selah* [pause, and calmly think of that]! ⁵ I lay down and slept; I wakened again, for the Lord sustains me.

It's not by might, nor by power, but by My Spirit. You cannot get to the top of this hill without divine intervention, for the root is infected. I have sent a divine intervention by My Holy Spirit and it hovers over you and brings you help from on high. You cannot do this in your might or will, you have reached a place in Me where you listen and receive My instruction and I will add no sorrow to it. I have gone before you and I have governed it. I have prepared the way and I have prepared those for you. I have sustained you, prepared you, and walked with you through these times for such a time as this. You bowed your head and submitted and I lifted your head, for I Am The Lifter of Your Head. Now, we go hand-in-hand collecting My gemstones all over the land. Arise, My beloved, for My Holy Spirit is hovering. It is movement time in the Spirit.

CHAPTER ONE

THE WILDERNESS

"Be careful. Stay on the path," I say to myself. "Just run. Do not think. Run!"

In the darkness of this desert night, a Hunter is growling, just off in the distance. It is loud enough for me to know I am the target, but far enough away to know it has not surrounded me, yet. My gut tells me to run, to trust my instincts and follow the path I know is before me, whether I see its outline clearly or not.

Run. Stop. Listen. Pant. Run again. Dodge all vegetation. Everything has thorns. Nothing is safe to touch.

"I have to climb!" I chastise myself, as I search the rocky cliffside for any place secure enough to support my weight. "Hurry, find a way up!" I have often hidden in small caves found in this cliffside. Without certainty that this is the right point for my ascent, I climb, "Just get out of the reach of the Hunters."

I have learned how to avoid the physical attacks of the Hunters, but there is no escaping their yipping, which has proven more lethal than their bites. Once the Hunters identify their prey, their yipping is a targeted serenade of condemnation and half-truths; proof-positive they are demonic in nature. Their bites are venomous, and leave their victims in a stupor of apathetic complacency. Hunters cannot just drag their victims off; victims have to cooperate with them. Once captured, most never find a way of escape. I did. I beat the odds, but I battle the Hunters every night.

"This time, I got lucky," I said to myself. I slipped into the shadows of a shallow cave, holding my breath to remain as silent as possible. Standing in the darkness of the cave, I looked down on the Hunters, directly below me, sniffing around the last place I stood on the desert floor. After a few minutes, they moved on, in search of other prey. I inhaled a breath of relief.

These days, I am usually just the observer, not because I am any different from other prodigals, but because I have learned how to avoid being the Hunted and how to mind my own business. That was not the case when I first entered the Wilderness. Occasionally, I stumbled across a prodigal, one still under the stupor of the Hunters, and offered to help. I shared what food I had, revealed the location of my shelter to them; but repeatedly, upon return from a day of gathering food, I found all of my belongings stolen. What started out as a genuine desire to help, turned into a cold-hearted 'they will have to learn the hard way' attitude within me. I was once a sacrificial giver, now I am a pale shadow of the 'me' before the dark night, as I have come to call it.

I sat on my heels with my back against the cave's wall, close to the entrance. I would be safe until morning if I stayed hidden. Something about this night felt reminiscent to the morning after I ran away from Papa, away from the Kingdom. My memory placed me at the highest point of the Eastern Pass again. It was as fresh in this moment as it was the day it happened. I was looking out over the vast Serpent's Valley as the morning sun spilled over the mountain's peaks. I had heard many stories about this barren wilderness, but that was the first time I had actually set eyes on it.

Papa's Kingdom is plush with wild flowers, herbs, and countless groves of olive and fruit trees. Massive shade trees line the streams of clear water. The temperature in the Kingdom is tolerable, unlike the Serpent's Valley, a barren and dry desert with soaring temperatures. The giant Saguaro Cacti almost looked human with their large arms bent toward the sky, telling me to stop. It never crossed my mind then, but I wondered now, if I felt captivated by them because Papa was trying to warn me, "turn back the way you came, and run home as fast as you can run." Hindsight is always clear sight, is it not?

The prickly pear and Cholla cacti spread across the desert floor as its only real greenery; the short shrubs were easy to look past since I was accustomed to towering trees. I remembered searching the horizon from that vantage point of the Eastern Pass and spying a grove of palm trees barely visible in the distance. Logic said it likely meant available water; had I known what the Oasis was really about, I would have walked right on past it. I did not have that privilege of wisdom at the time. All I had was a naïve belief that a new life waited for me in the Plains of Carnal Pleasure. It was not a life of the Kingdom, but I was certain I could find something to numb my pain and silence my grief. As I judged the distance between that palm grove of the Oasis and the Eastern Pass, I figured it would take me from sunrise to sunset to reach it. The Oasis was not my final destination, but it was a good stopping point to rest overnight on my journey to the Plains of Carnal Pleasure.

That first fateful day, I walked among the thorns of the desert ignorant to the Hunters; I thought my greatest challenge would be finding water. I learned the hard way that everything in the Serpent's Valley was hostile, literally everything.

The first time I heard the yipping of the Hunters, I assumed they were coyotes. The first time I saw Hunters, I thought they were some breed of jackal, just much larger. Hunters are not animals at all; they are demonic hybrids of some kind who are restricted to the Valley's desert floor. Their yips are a language, a voice of darkness personalized to the Hunted.

Hunters are well trained, battle-worn opponents who use the intelligence gathered by other unclean spirits to strike victims with condemnation. Their verbal attacks were so precise, they could disable a human's defenses in a few sentences. "Where is your God, Mat'ta? Does He search for you? Obviously not, I found you so easily. Is He lost or just late… again? No matter, I am here and He is not." The questions were accusations, and an affront to my mind. Before these accusations, I did not doubt the goodness of God. After these questions, that is all I did: accuse God for everything hard or wrong in my life.

"Does He really protect you? Do you need protecting, Mat'ta? After all, you did willingly walk away. You chose to wander into the forbidden Serpent's Valley." The yips multiplied, along with the accusations and questions, as additional Hunters joined in on the attack. "What are you searching for, Mat'ta? We know the answer is 'more'… You are searching for more of what, exactly; more than God has been for you, or is it as simple as relief from His burdensome requirements of holiness? Was Papa unable to make you righteous, to make you WANT to be righteous?"

It was true. I came into the Wilderness looking for relief from my grief, but until this very moment, I had not discerned my doubts about what Papa required of my behavior. In agreement with the Hunter's condemnation, I made my own declaration, "I always feel like a disappointment to Papa. I am never enough, and to be honest, I just do not have the energy to care anymore." This cooperation with darkness proved to be spiritually costly.

"Are you wondering where all the power is, or where all the miracles are in your life? Maybe you are not praying right, or maybe He has not chosen you, at least not for important things." On and on the voices went. The more I listened, the more it sounded like my own voice and less like the yipping of the Hunters, the very evidence that the Hunters had the upper hand in this battle.

By the time I reached the Oasis, my spirit felt tortured, even betrayed by my soul. I had not intended on agreeing with the voices of the Hunters. My spirit protested; it brought scriptures of promise and comfort to memory, but as these questions took on life as accusations, doubts swirled like dust devils along the surface of the sterile places in my soul. My ignorance and spiritual immaturity reinforced these doubts about Papa's goodness. My cooperation with the Hunter's accusations sliced at my spirit and wounded my faith. My spirit was crying out, "choke the life out of that Hunter, and crush his head under your heel! Resist his lies!" but my soul rebutted, "What lies? What part is untrue? Look at your life. Look at what is true."

My wounded spirit acquiesced to my soul's logic, and without understanding at the time, logic was the missing additive for the destruction of my child-like faith. Tentacles of darkness broke through the surface of my Garden of Faith, wrapped themselves around the trunk of every planting of the Word of God, and began the slow drip of poisonous accusation and doubt into the soil of my mind. My wounded spirit proved impotent to stop the caustic ooze from penetrating my emotions through the cracks of offense. All of the barren, sterile places in the womb of my soul absorbed the poison, making it hostile to the seed of Spiritual Life. Every agreement with Darkness, as slight as each might be, aborted the Seeds of Faith. As Faith died, the 'evidence of things hoped for' vanished, and only what 'could be seen or proven' survived; no supernatural power, no ability to hear, or see, or perceive the Presence of God. Papa's voice grew silent.

Connie Hartzler / Mat'ta

Weakened under hostile physical and spiritual conditions, I lived at the Oasis in a state of defeat and apathy for quite some time. I ate the grapes from the vine; I gathered any low-bearing fruit on the trees. I drank from the natural springs. I could not hear Papa, but somehow, I wanted to believe He made a way for me in the desert. Early on, The Holy Spirit wooed me, urged me to pray and worship and tend the Garden. Literally, I felt compelled to turn the soil, to uproot weeds, to find a way to haul water to distant plantings. I did all this at first, but less and less over time. The work was hard. On hot days, or I-don't-feel-like-it days, I rationalized away the urgency. I had all I needed: Food, water, cool shade. I barely noticed when some vines became barren for lack of pruning. Over time, because I neglected the work, and frankly, became lazy, the Garden of Faith withered. In its place, new saplings sprung up. They grew at an accelerated pace, which seemed to directly correlate to my neglect of the Garden. The more complacent and lazier I became, the faster the saplings grew. One sapling became the Tree of Doubt, and another the Tree of Mistrust. One grew to be a tall Cypress called Accusation. The one I most frequently claimed, as a place of solace, was the large Mesquite Tree called Judgment.

The Garden of Faith withered and transformed into thistle and tumbleweeds; in contrast, the shade and protection of the new

Trees became more and more attractive; however, rest under the canopy of The Trees of Darkness came at a great price. Any short time of relief from the heat meant exposure to the aroma of the Trees, which brought mental dullness, apathy, and unreasonable suspicion. To complicate the situation, The Winds of Darkness whirled around these trees with more logical reasoning and strengthened arguments and challenged the goodness of God. My spirit heard the songs of Winds as the irresistible song of a Siren.

"Would I ever be free from the Serpent's voice? Is a renewed mind even possible anymore?" In this environment, those two thoughts were foreign. They came from a source other than the Trees or Winds of Darkness; they were the dying breaths of my own spirit begging for its life.

The thoughts stirred desperation within me. I knew I had to reach the bubbling spring, to drink from its fresh water, if my spirit had any hope of survival. I literally crawled on my hands and knees in search of the natural spring until I found only a bubbling above the ground. There was no longer a pool to lie in, only a small muddy fountain of water remained. The source of life was nearly gone. The circumstances were hopeless.

My head was foggy, but my spirit began to weep tears of desperate pleading and surrender. As these tears rolled from my face and mingled with the bubbling spring, the fountain grew in strength and force. Soon, I could drink long gulps of cool, clean water. Once my deep thirst was satisfied, I felt a familiar tug on my conscience: the tug of conviction for sin. Conviction was once a burden to my soul, but in this state of deprivation, it was a sign of hope for my spirit. For the first time since I could recall, the will of my spirit overpowered my soul as I lay in the renewed springs and whispered, "Papa, can you even see me? Can I come home?"

As soon as I had the physical strength to run, I escaped the Oasis. The Hunters chased me relentlessly. It was in this time of constant attack I discovered that they could only reach me if I remained on the desert floor. For months, maybe a year, I searched for the path that led back to the Kingdom, but out of fear of the Hunters, I ended up in a cave before sunset. My resolve to return to Papa remained strong, but my confidence that I would make it home began a slow fade.

That is how it has been, until now. Yipping and growls off in the distance interrupted my reminiscing and yanked my mind back to the present reality; but much closer, maybe only a few dozen yards, I heard screams and whimpers of very young children. At first, I thought my mind was playing tricks on me, but when a distinct "Mama!" from a young infant echoed through the valley; there was no mistaking what I heard. The children's voices yanked and pulled my mother's heart in their direction as if there was an invisible chain between them and me. Better instincts told me to find cover, but instead I readied my spear and slingshot, in preparation to find those children...before it was too late. I pleaded and bargained with God as I hastily worked, "Papa, I know we have a lot to work out between us, but right now...right now in this moment...there's a child crying out for her Mama...in the Serpent's Valley. What are children doing in the Serpent's Valley?"

As clear as my own voice I heard the Holy Spirit's response, "Yes, Mat'ta, why is my child in the Serpent's Valley?" He meant me. I knew His voice.

"I am trying to get home, Papa. Right now, please help me." Right now, I have a problem bigger than my own sense of spiritual dullness, so I beg, "Please, Papa, please just tell me what to do. I do not want to die. I don't want these children to die..."

Papa interrupted, "climb to the ridge above you, but keep your eye on the desert floor. Stay low, and move among the Desert

Broom, not out in the open." As long as I remained undetected, the Hunters remained restricted to the desert floor below me. If I alerted them to my location, they were free to pursue me by way of the foothills just a few miles from here. Stealth was my safety.

In the invisible realm, Ma'oz, my Guardian Angel, was already at my shoulder. The very second I whispered Papa's name at the Oasis, Ma'oz was assigned as my angelic protector. Ma'oz has Papa's instructions to follow; the primary one is 'do not make your presence known to her'. Like all guardians, they fulfill their created purpose by serving their assigned humans, but unless given permission by God, they are not to bring attention to themselves. In this way, guardians keep their abode and remain submitted to Papa. Discerning believers are capable of sensing the presence of angels and unclean spirits; but in the dull condition I found myself, all I discerned was Papa's still small voice. In the visible realm, I have my own skill, my physical strength, a homemade spear, and a slingshot I found on the desert floor months ago. My hope was that Papa and the angels of God were with me. "Okay, Papa, here we go," I said to myself as I took one big breath and exhaled; I climbed among the boulders and crags as I moved up the cliffside trying not to lose my footing on the caliche surface.

"Slow Mat'ta, be very quiet," Ma'oz says aloud. I could not hear him, but I felt the encouragement in my spirit.

As I got my feet under me as I gained my balance on the top of the ridge, I heard the cry of a young baby, and then I heard the familiar yip of the Hunters much closer than before.

"No, Papa, not the children, please!" I begged in a harsh whisper. The children were on the desert floor. From my vantage point of the ridge, it appeared there were eight children of various ages. The older boys were taking a defensive stance with sticks. The eldest girl held the baby, and huddled the two other small children in the center of the circle. All of them were frightened and panicked. I climbed down the ridge, set my footing, stopped to load my sling, and then shot a rock-bullet from my sling. Practice had paid off. I hit the Alpha Hunter square in the side of the head, knocking it off its feet. Two more accurately placed shots, and the Hunter stopped its yipping and ran off in a scurry. I stood my ground, poised with my slingshot loaded for more shots because there is never just one Hunter. Three others stopped their pursuit several yards back from the children, watched their leader scurry off, paused in what appeared to be confusion, and then followed close behind the Alpha Hunter. The pack of Hunters was gone. The window of opportunity for escape was right now.

I continued the descent until I was just a few yards away from the frightened huddle of bodies. I tried to speak in a calm, quiet, unthreatening tone as I said, "it is okay. I will not hurt you. I hit the Hunter with three shots. It ran off, but you do not have a lot of time. I know you're scared..." I put my sling in its place at the small of my back, secured next to my spear.

The oldest boy stepped forward with a large stick pointed at me, which shook in his hand from the surge of adrenaline. The oldest girl held the infant on her right hip, and controlled the toddlers with her left. She pushed them behind her back to place herself between us. The other three boys, sticks in hand, joined the eldest to form a larger wall of defense, trying to look braver than they actually were. None of them spoke, except the infant, who said "Mama." At first, I thought the baby's gibber was endearing but as she strained against her sister's grip to turn in my direction, her single word became more desperate, "Mama!" This curly headed, blue-eyed angel put her hands out to reach in my direction. Every atom of my being wanted to take her into my arms and comfort her. Her insistent recognition of me, completely given over to her belief that I was, in fact, her mother was unsettling. When I saw the countenance of the older children change as well, it startled me; nonetheless, I stood firm in my insistence to help and spoke in soft tones, "please, don't be frightened. I have a safe place for you, but you must come now, right now."

In the invisible realm, Etsem and Qayam, two additional angelic warriors, joined Ma'oz. Together, the three angels spread their wings and cloaked the whole group of us, using their angelic bodies as mirrored surfaces, which reflected the desert back upon itself. Under the protective wings of the guardians, we were safe and hidden from the sight of any predator, especially the Hunters.

The eldest girl said, "we'll come with you." Holding the infant on one hip, she stepped forward first to follow me. The twin toddlers, a boy and a girl, followed closely behind, then the three boys, and finally the eldest boy brought up the rear.

"Stay silent. Follow closely. Walk exactly where I walk." We moved quickly along the desert floor being careful not to brush up against any bushes or cacti; any disturbance in the vegetation could alert the Hunters of our location. We followed the markings I placed on several Saguaros to maneuver several hundred yards before I stopped the group. This time I was certain of my location. I pointed directly in front of me and asked in a whisper, "do you see that rock wall?" I waited for a response from the two eldest siblings. "Do you see the darker shadow near the top? That is my home. It is a shallow cave. It is warm, dry, and perfectly safe. You can rest there." Everyone nodded his or her head in understanding and agreement. When we were directly below the cave, I indicated to all of the middle boys that they needed to start climbing. I spoke specifically to the redheaded boy, "when you get to the opening in the cave, you will see a basket with a rope. Lower it to us. I will place the baby in the basket and climb the cliffside with her myself. You'll need to pull the basket up as I climb, okay?"

I instructed the two oldest children to remove their outer shirts. I showed them how to tie them around their waist and shoulders as a sling to support the weight of their toddler siblings. Once they felt the children were secure, I instructed them to begin the climb up to the cave. "Hurry," I said, then I leaned over each toddler and whispered, "hold on as tight as you can!"

Moments later, the basket tumbled down the cliffside. I placed the baby in the basket, secured my weapons as I always did, and started the climb with the baby. I lifted the basket with the baby over the edge and slid it away from me. As I climbed over the cliff's edge, I heard the eldest girl comforting the younger children, speaking soft words of assurance that Papa knows where they are, and He would protect them. She retrieved the baby from the basket and snuggled her head against her own neck, but the baby resisted her comfort and reached over her shoulder toward me.

With her arms stretched out, she said, "Mama!" and cried a demanding cry for me to take her. I asked the young woman for permission to take the infant from her arms, and then I said, "you are very gentle and loving with your siblings. I can see you care very deeply for their well-being. You bear a lot of responsibility, but it's obvious you do quite well."

She smiled a bright smile and said, "Thank you."

In the same moment, the infant girl smiled at me and said, "Mama." My eyes welled with tears as an involuntary response to the baby. I looked at the older girl with a searching for some answer as to why the baby continued to call me Mama. She simply smiled and shrugged her shoulder.

The toddlers had moved toward me, one to each side, wrapped their hands around the inside of my knees and leaned their heads on my thigh. Their fearless confidence in me stunned my heart. Why do they act as if they know me? Why does my own heart behave as if I know them? The eldest boy then moved next to me. He smiled.

Now that everyone was safe from harm's way, I said, "we'll

have plenty of time to talk tomorrow. For right now, go lie down and sleep. I'll keep guard." Everyone obeyed without any hesitation, lying next to or on top of another; and all were asleep in a matter of a couple of breaths. I sat in the opening of the cave with my back against the wall at the entrance.

Yip... Yip... First the outcry came, then the growl, and then finally the silence. The Hunters found their nightly prey. I looked back at the sleeping children with a deep sigh, "thank you, Papa, for saving us. What now?" I did not hear an answer, but I felt one in my heart, "one day at a time."

Ma'oz, meaning 'Fortified', named as such because of his sheer size, stood twenty feet tall and six feet wide. His presence was a message to the invisible realm, one that declared 'God is Mat'ta's protection'. Words were not necessary, only his presence as he stood on the peak of the cliff above the cave entrance. Qayam, meaning 'Steadfast', and Etsem, meaning 'Strong Body', also angels of massive size, stood with Ma'oz on the peak. Ma'oz often guards Mat'ta alone, but for this assignment, Papa sent high-ranking reinforcements. Qayam, a General in the Lord's army, assigned to the Serpent's Valley as leader of the angelic troops who watch over the prodigals. Etsem is one of his Captains, as is Ma'oz.

Ma'oz asked General Qayam, "what are the instructions of the Lord of Hosts?"

The General sat in silence for a moment. Ma'oz and Etsem waited for his response.

"That will be determined by the choices of Mat'ta. Papa desires for all of them to survive this. Mat'ta's broken heart clouds her judgment. We must do what we are commanded: guard and protect the children until they arrive home. Ma'oz, you will live up to your name before this is over. You will be Mat'ta's fortified protection today." Ma'oz nodded his head in agreement as he spoke quietly to Papa in his own mind, "Papa, please stir the humans to pray."

The two eldest children each lie still with their eyes closed as they prayed for protection for the several siblings tucked under their arms. Within moments, they were soundly asleep.

Hours later, as the sun rose, streaks of orange and pink colored the surface of everything in the desert, and greeted my soul with Papa's unmistakable, "Good Morning, Beloved," just as it did when I lived in the kingdom. "It's a new day dawning in my life," I said to myself under my breath. As the morning sun filled the cave, the eldest two children awoke. Occupied with peeling the skin off a couple dozen prickly pears, I barely noticed when they both moved toward me to watch my efforts. The preparation of prickly pear fruit can be daunting. The hair-like needles cover the exterior of the fruit. Removing the skin and needles without contaminating the edible insides took practice. Once it was done, the rest of the preparation of grinding the inside fruit into a drinkable puree was very simple.

"Good morning." I said as I continued the grinding.

Both responded with a smile and a return "good morning."

I said, "my name is Mat'ta," letting the sentence dangle with an opening to indicate I was hoping for a return introduction.

"I'm Rachel. This is Michael," she said as she leaned in closer with obvious interest in what I was doing. Michael remained silent but was less guarded in his body language than he had been in the beginning.

"In a moment, I will finish filling this bowl. You can all take turns drinking from it," I said as I sipped a taste for myself to test the texture.

Rachel looked around the cave entrance at the hand-made

utensils and weapons. Then she noticed the bark bowl full of seeds.

"Those are ironwood seeds. I've roasted them already…go ahead and taste some." Rachel dipped her hand into the seeds and popped a couple in her mouth, then offered her full hand to her brother who did the same. Both returned a wide-eyed approval as they chewed the seeds.

"They taste good, huh?" I said as they confirmed with strong nods of approval.

"Rachel, use that bowl and the mallet to grind up the mesquite seeds," I said, as I pointed to her right. She reached for the bowl and mallet and moved closer to the pile of mesquite pods. She broke open a pod to find a short row of seeds, which she dumped into the bowl. Michael moved toward her to help. They worked together, mostly in silence. When the bowl was half-full, I moved toward the two of them to show Rachel how to use the mallet to grind the seeds. She caught on to the task very quickly. Michael continued peeling pods.

"The rain is coming. The sunrise lit the ceiling of clouds on fire this morning, but that will be the last of the sun we see for today. Can you smell the creosote?" I inhaled deeply. Wet creosote has a very distinct fragrance, one that has come to trigger the feeling of relief within me, relief from the heat, relief from thirst. The fragrance of creosote was a sign of hope.

"It must already be raining on the other side of this ridge." I said.

For the first time in a very long time a scripture ran through my mind, "whoever drinks of the water that I shall give him shall never thirst. That water will spring up into everlasting life." It was Christ's response to the woman at the well. My heart felt sorrow and warmth at the same time with the recognition of the scripture. I related to the Samaritan woman. She, too, knew regret... brokenness... and isolation, but she also knew the son of God, and He changed everything.

Ma'oz and the other two angels recognized that the Holy Spirit was speaking to Mat'ta openly as she contemplated the scriptures. In the spiritual realm, her response to the Holy Spirit manifested as a bolt of light shooting from her heart out into the heavenlies, and traveled with a humming sound. It was of the same frequency as the hum that emanated from the heart of The Lord of Host, which meant He was near. Ma'oz moved from the peak of the cliff to the opening of the cave where he sensed the presence of the Holy Spirit with Mat'ta. He readied himself to respond to any command from the Lord of Hosts, but reveled in the privilege of witnessing The Holy Spirit's playful dancing around the younger children as they woke from their nightly sleep. He moved gently among them, swirling in and out, greeting each with a morning hug. The three middle boys yawned and stretched. One reached over to pick up the infant and put her in his lap. The toddlers stood up and moved closer to Rachel to gaze over her shoulder in curiosity of what she was doing.

"Good morning, everyone, breakfast will be ready very soon." I mixed a little of the prickly pear puree with the ground meal from the mesquite seeds to form small cakes, then moved toward the small fire pit. It held embers from the day before, which heated the flat cooking rocks warm enough to brown the small cakes. The toddlers followed me, full of curiosity and trusting innocence, to the fire's edge. Once the cakes browned, I scooped them into a bark bowl using my flat make-shift-spatula-stick, and then I blew on the cakes to cool them. The toddlers leaned over the bowl to help, spitting more than blowing. Their sincere effort to help warmed my heart. I could not keep myself from kissing each child's forehead. They both looked at me with big grins and leaned their cheeks toward me as a request for more kisses. I wholeheartedly obliged with playful embraces as I kissed their eyes, cheeks, and forehead.

All three of us squealed in delight.

My heart felt full for the first time in years; yet tears stung my eyes as thoughts of my own children flooded my mind. My twins would have been about this age by now. Losing them to miscarriage devastated me. Their deaths were the beginning of my spiritual spiral into the dark night. Theirs had not been the first pregnancy lost to miscarriage, but it was the most devastating. A year after physically recovering from that miscarriage, but utterly full of bitter pain, I left the Kingdom without warning. I left my husband, our home, and our life without any explanation. The fear of facing the consequences of that choice kept me from returning. I knew my husband would search for me, but a year was a long time. His own pain from the repeated miscarriages was devastating; my abandonment surely intensified it. My heart was so offended and stiff with grief; the last words I spoke were intentionally mean to make leaving easier. Could I return and face all of that? Would there be anything left of my marriage or home to salvage? Did God kill my kids or did he allow the devil to steal them? Regardless, I could not reconcile how a loving God could do either, so trusting him with anything else seemed risky as well. That was how offense took me captive. That is when I bought into the belief, I was better off figuring life out for myself; that is when I became a prodigal with a rebellious determination to live a life in the Plains of Carnal Pleasure, where I could numb my reality.

The two little ones looked up from the cakes and said, "hot. Hot." Their sweet little voices jerked my spiraling emotions back to the moment at hand.

"Yes, hot." I responded. I tore one cooled cake in half and gave each child a piece. It was a little bitter, but their hunger overpowered their taste buds, and within a few moments, they were asking for more. By now, the three middle children had joined us, and were giggling at the facial expressions the toddlers made because of the bitterness of the cakes. The laughter of the three boys goaded the toddlers to over-exaggerate their expressions, which in turn, encouraged more laughter. When the three boys each took a cooled cake from the bowl and tasted it with caution, they too made silly faces spawned by the cake's bitterness, but eventually, they devoured all they were served.

I looked at Rachel and Michael and asked, "how long has it been since you all had a meal?"

"Not since we left Flamingo Paradise a couple days ago," she answered as she shifted the weight of the infant from one hip to the other.

"What is her name, Rachel?" I asked.

I watched Rachel dip her finger into the prickly pear puree and put it in the baby's mouth for her to suck on. She patiently fed the baby this way until she seemed satisfied.

"Her name is Elizabeth." She responded.

Meanwhile, Michael gave each of the older boys a handful of ironwood seeds as he said, "chew 'em. They're really good," as he encouraged them to eat the seeds instead of the cakes. Michael was also wiser than his age, and more grown up than any young man should have to be. I noticed he did not eat any of the cakes himself; he left them for the smaller children who would find them easier to eat. The toddlers went to Michael to beg for their own seeds. He bit one in half and gave each one a piece, making sure they could handle the seed without choking. When they did so, he let them have a small handful each.

"Michael, what are their names?" I asked.

He answered, "Thomas and Tasha. But we call Thomas 'T' for short because that's what Tasha calls him."

I gasped and put my hand over my mouth all in one involuntary movement. I had chosen these names for my own twins. What are the chances of that? Thomas and Tasha moved toward me as I offered each another small cake.

"My name is Mat'ta," I said to the toddlers, putting an emphasis on the 'T'.

Both enunciated "Mama" with an emphasis on the 'M'.

I repeated, "No, Mat'ta" with more of an emphasis on the 'T'.

They repeated "Mama" with just as much of an emphasis on the 'M'.

Without hesitation, but with all the innocence of children, they both wrapped their arms around my neck and put their head on each shoulder. I wept with my eyes closed. Many days I grieved longing to hear my own children call me "Mama." Somehow, in this moment, these two little strangers were knitting my broken heart back together with their silky little voices, and the soft touch of their little chubby fingers. Michael waited until I opened my eyes and caught his intense gaze. "You are Mama," Michael said as a declaration. He nodded his own head with a smile.

Strengthened by spoken truth, General Qayam, Captains Ma'oz and Etsem, all filled with bright holy light as Michael spoke "You are Mama." The truth was coming out of the shadows of the 'unrecognized' into the open as 'possibility' in Mat'ta's heart. This reality caused the angels to illuminate as brightly as if a star had fallen from the sky and landed at the opening in the cave. Papa stood in the tower of His palace gazing intently in the direction of the cave. When he saw the light from His warriors, He rejoiced and danced with such abandon, He had to lift His robe to keep from tripping on it. All the while, He repeatedly sang, "My Beloved, Mat'ta!"

CHAPTER TWO

AWAKENING

The rain came in monsoon force. Everyone backed into the cave to get out of the storm. There was no lightning in the storm, just heavy rain so I moved out of the cave, sat on the rocks, and let the downpour wash over me. All of the children joined me, except Elizabeth; she was sound asleep in the shadows of the cave, suckling her bottom lip rhythmically as all infants do in their sleep. As I lie flat on my back with my mouth wide open, heavy rain filled up my mouth. I swallowed gulps of water. The kids imitated my actions, but animated their effort with giggles and squeals of delight. I giggled right along with them at the simple pleasures of a rainstorm.

Another memory flooded my mind of a special night during a monsoon storm. My husband, Noel, had arranged for a magnificent evening of luxurious dining, harp music included, as a special touch to our celebration. The monsoon that evening was producing a brilliant lightning show with dozens of strikes per minute. We were safe inside the walls of Papa's Kingdom, high in the city business towers, with a spectacular view of the valley and the mountains. It was a special occasion for us, especially with dear friends serving the dinner. At that time in life, our love affair was so full of youthful passion and intensity people frequently told us they could feel the chemistry between us. This was especially true on this night. From the very beginning, since we were young teenagers, people marveled at the depth of our relationship.

"You are made for each other," our server said. We were accustomed to that saying because Papa used to say it with such pleasure. Remembering young love was the Holy Spirit wooing me in this present moment.

"Papa, I love him. I do. I have harmed him so deeply…" I said to myself as I thought on that memory of the most precious person in my life.

Then, with stark clarity, Papa spoke directly to my spirit, "he has been looking for you for a year. Even now, he is searching and still believing you are alive. He was devastated, Mat'ta, ruined actually. He could not comprehend how or why you would abandon him. He spent months in grief until brokenness came; when it did, he broke in the right places. I have renamed him Braveheart, Mat'ta, a man of stout character. He does not pretend, Beloved, you know this. He may have strong words when he finds you, but you must know that he loves you with an unending love. He loves you like I do, Mat'ta." This was definitely Papa speaking to my spirit and he was definitely talking about my man. Suddenly, I surged with a hope I had not felt in a very long time.

Squeals of pleasure jerked me back to the moment at hand. The rain was still coming down in a steady flow as the children danced around and pounced from one puddle to the next. Rachel was ruffling the hair of every boy as the rain poured over them. They thought she was playing; I knew she was washing as much debris from their scalp as possible.

"Please let the rain keep coming, Lord. These boys stink like the stink of stinky boys. They need a bath. Peter, John-Mark, and Timothy shake your head like a wet dog, like this…" Rachel said as she bent over at the waist and shook her head until her hair flew all around her. "Take your shirts off and scrub your skin with them, especially your silly faces." The toddlers and Michael also got in on the fun, and for that moment, they had no cares in the world.

Baby Elizabeth began stirring with just the beginnings of a whimper. I stood and stepped inside the cave to reach for her as she greeted me with her world-shattering "Mama." I picked her up and kissed her cheek as I said, "Mat'ta" very clearly and slowly. She squealed with delight, and then reached for Rachel as I approached the entrance of the cave. I whispered to Rachel as she took the baby from my arms, "you and your family have changed my life. Thank you."

"I know. That's why we came," Rachel replied.

"What do you mean?" I asked because her answer did not make sense to me.

"That's why we left Flamingo Paradise two days ago to find you. Papa said you desperately needed us. So we came," Rachel replied.

"What?" I asked, stunned.

Two days ago, I lay in this cave in a state of despair and hopelessness, comforting myself with thoughts of death. I had said to myself, "I'd rather be where they are. I want to be with my kids." I meant heaven. I meant death. I meant... many things. Rachel saw the confusion and disbelief in my face, and then answered me as if she could read my mind.

"I know. Papa knew you needed us. He sent us to find you. Do you know who we are?" Rachel spoke the pivotal question, the one question that Papa intended to use to shift my history. I was afraid to say anything, but there was no mistaking the truth. Rachel looked exactly like me when I was her age. She was my oldest child. The rest of the children were mine as well, right down to baby Elizabeth.

"Yes, I know who you are. I don't know how you are here, but I am desperately grateful that you are," I said as I embraced them both so tightly Rachel struggled to breathe, but she still managed to say, "I love you, Mama."

I pulled back just enough to look Elizabeth in the eyes. Elizabeth died in the Serpent's Valley, at the Oasis, shortly after I left the Kingdom. She is the exact age now as the amount of time since that horrendous loss. "How is this possible?" I asked as I wept in heaves; purifying heaves. It was the cry I was afraid would never end if I ever allowed it to get started. Rachel just held me in a gentle embrace with Elizabeth between us. There was a silence between us for several minutes. The other children heard my crying and came to comfort me. Thomas and Tasha wrapped their arms around my knees; Peter, John-Mark, and Timothy formed a circle around us as Michael leaned over my left shoulder, "we all love you so much, Mama. We don't mind waiting for you… we'll see you again." My empty arms were full. Papa knew how much I needed my arms filled with my own children. He knew.

Rachel said, "Mama, you came into this wretched valley to hunt down the Serpent because you believed he stole us from you. We have not been in the Valley of the Serpent. We have been in Flamingo Paradise… perfectly safe…. along with all the children who live there. No one is sad, Mama, and we're together." She waited patiently as my sobs spoke their intelligible language of pain. When I calmed a bit, she continued, "there's something else, Mama. Papa wants me to tell you that this territory belongs to the Serpent. The rebellious prodigals forfeit their spiritual authority to him when they choose his ways and believe his lies. He has no authority of his own, but he does not waste authority given to him willingly. You cannot win a battle against him. The only one who can win your war is The Lord of Hosts and his angelic army. Papa wants your suffering to end, Mama."

My heart knew this was truth. I nodded my head in agreement, "so do I Sweet Child."

Elizabeth reached for me. As I took her in my arms, she wrapped her soft little hands around my neck. I kissed her head as she responded, "Mama."

"Yes, baby girl, Mama." I replied.

I took each of the other children in my arms, one sweet boy at a time, and held them as I spoke how much I love them. When I got to Michael he said, "please choose life… please go home…" The strength and genuine compassion of his embrace absorbed the burning pain I felt in my chest. I opened my eyes to look up at him, but it was no longer Michael. In that split moment, I saw Jesus.

My body shook and startled at the loud clap of thunder. I sat up and looked around for the children. I was alone. My reality hit me. It had all been a dream.

My body heaved with sobs as I screamed a moan that only Holy Spirit could interpret. He did. He washed over me like waves of the sea as I rocked on my knees with my head in my hands. The storehouses of grief within my soul burst open like a dam overwhelmed with floodwaters. There was no stopping the outpouring of mourning from my spirit. As each tear fell, Holy Spirit caught it in His hand, and threw it toward the heavens. As it hit the sky, it shattered like crystal, but remained suspended. When my sobbing stopped, and I took in a deep breath out of sheer exhaustion, Holy Spirit had created a masterpiece with the suspended fragments of my tears in the shape of Papa's face expressing such agonizing grief, it caused Ma'oz, Qayam, and Etsem to moan in despair as they peered at its majesty. I could not see the masterpiece of the Holy Spirit, but I could sense it. I felt it. I felt Him. I knew in my spirit that God was for me and not against me. I knew He loved me.

"Papa, I want to live. I must live." I repeated my thought aloud.

CHAPTER THREE

BRAVEHEART

Noel heard the thunder clap. It was so violent and loud; he assumed the lightning strike must have been very close. He climbed the ridge to look for fire, but was stunned to silence and stillness when he heard the heart wrenching scream and moan of a woman. He looked down the cliffside to witness the breaking of a human spirit. There before him was a woman grieving so thoroughly, so openly, he said to himself, "this woman is at her end." The thought occurred to him, either the breaking was unto life or … she would not fight to live much longer. That thought hooked his spirit with compassion and a deep "I-know-this-pain" recognition that compelled him to help her. It would derail his mission to find Mat'ta. For only a moment, he weighed the contradictory choices in his logical mind: help her or back away and go around the ridge another way. In the end, there was no choice. He would help her. That is what honor tells him to do.

Noel began the decent down the cliffside. As the rain began pouring so heavily, he could hardly hear his own scream, "Hello! I'm coming to help you!"

He was half way down the cliff when his screams hit my ears…" Hello! I'm coming to help you!" I stood to my feet, moved to get a better vantage point and a look at the ascending stranger headed in my direction. I quickly turned back to the cave entrance and grabbed my spear. I backed myself into the darkened edges. I had the advantage because I knew this cave. He would have no idea what he was stepping into…

Noel announced himself, "Hello?" but stood just out of the downpour under the cliff's natural overhang over the cave entrance, "I'm here to help you. I heard your outcry before the rain started." Noel put his back against the cave entrance and slid down into a squat. His body language spoke more than his words: worn out and physically exhausted. The slump in his shoulders said something else: Heartbroken. I know this man. "I know you, Noel, I see you." I thought to myself. Everything in my heart scrambled. Excitement, fear, shame and deep, deep love competed for attention. I let it all flow forward, but I did not move.

"I heard your moan. I heard you break. I have been in this pain myself. I don't know what I can do, but I'm here to help you." He never looked into the cave. It was too dark to see anything defining anyway. He just talked believing someone was listening. He dropped his body the remainder of the distance until his bottom rested on the floor of the cave. He kept his knees bent; put his elbows on his knees, and his head in his hands. He did not say another word for several minutes. When there was no response, he let his legs straighten, and put his head back against the cave wall as he looked out at the downpour. "If you don't mind, I'll just rest here for a moment until the rain stops… then I'll go."

I had already begun moving in his direction. When I was in the light enough for him to recognize me, I said his name, "Noel."

His was instantly on his feet with as much surprise in his body as there was in the expression on his face. "Mat'ta?"

I rushed into his arms as he enveloped me without hesitation. We stood in that embrace for a moment, then I started to say, "Noel, I'm so sorry…" He put his hand over my mouth to stop my words. He shook his head 'no' but said nothing. He drew me back into another reassuring embrace, and then dropped his arms as he stepped out of the cave. I knew he was overcome with conflicting emotion; he is such a measured thinker; I knew he was considering his words and his actions. I also knew better than to step past the invisible boundaries he just put in place. I stood in my own space, lost in my own conflicting emotion, and I waited in the silence.

Moments later, I stepped toward the cave's wall to lean my spear against it. Without looking at me, he said, "you'll need that." I answered, "I know, but not right now, and not with you." He turned and looked at me. All in one moment, the pain of all our loss flooded between us. Tears filled both of our eyes. I could not stand apart from him, not one more second; I leapt forward and threw my arms around his head, as his arms encompassed me.

"You found me." I whispered.

"I never lost you. You lost you." He answered. "I just came to take you home."

In the invisible realm, Gibbor, Noel's Guardian Angel, whose name means 'Mighty', along with Ma'oz, drew arrows from their quiver, loaded their bows, and shot the arrows in the direction of the Oasis. These arrows streaked through the sky with a frequency hum that sounded like a trumpet. They were a signal to the Lord of Hosts: "Mission accomplished."

In the earthly realm, two lightning bolts merged as they struck the desert floor. It was a precise hit as it split a large mesquite tree in half, and instantly incinerated the roots. The Lord of Hosts and his angelic warriors stood at that exact mesquite tree to witness the precise marksmanship of His Angelic Captains. Jesus, clothed in His great armor and robe of righteousness, shot an arrow with his own bow, this one toward the Palace. Sentinel angels carried the message through the treetops until Papa received it: "Mission accomplished."

Once Jesus sent the message to Papa, He stepped closer to the burning tree trunk, and spoke the curse he once spoke over a fig tree: "May no men eat from the fruit of this tree, forevermore." The angelic realm did not question the Lord's commanding curse; every angel knew the mesquite was not fruit bearing, nor was it an ordinary mesquite. They watched intently as the Lord turned to the other three remaining trees and spoke the same curse. All four Trees of Darkness instantly withered. As the last leaf or needle fell from its branches, the angelic army could hear a discernible exhale from each tree. They were more than trees. Jesus then walked over to the bubbling spring and thanked Papa for His mercy. The spring responded with a fountain tall enough for Jesus to take a long drink. Once His thirst was satisfied, He said, "Spring up, O Well!" With that command, a geyser shot several dozen feet into the air. The barren desert where the Oasis once flourished flooded afresh. The army of God shouted in unison, "victory to the King of Kings!"

The Lord of Hosts shouted into the Heavens, "let it be known, let it be witnessed, the Serpent's Trees are dead!" In the natural realm, the Lord's declaration manifested as a thunderclap that reverberated so loudly it shook the mountainside. Noel and I both jumped in a startle. "That was more than a thunderclap. That was a message," Noel said.

Ma'oz illuminated with holy light and drew his sword all in one movement. He instantly discerned the encroaching presence of the Serpent. On the desert floor, directly below the cave, the demonic prince of the Valley coiled its body, raised its head, and rattled its tail in preparation to strike at the humans. This Serpent, of formidable size, was the territorial demon that controlled the Serpent's Valley. It raised itself with its neck taut, head drawn back, and fangs exposed until it was at even height with the opening of the cave. General Qayam and Captain Etsem joined Ma'oz and Gibbor at the cave's entrance with their weapons drawn. All were prepared for battle if it came to that.

Noel intuitively sensed the disturbance to the peace in the spiritual realm. He stepped to the cliff's edge, and unknowingly walked through Qayam's translucent body. He held on to the rim of his hat as he leaned into the wind that whipped up and over the side of the cliff. Noel could not see the Serpent, but it stood only inches from his face, hissing so intensely the tendons in its neck bulged. The Serpent could not touch Noel, but said in a human voice, "Praying Man" with hatred and disdain in its tone.

Noel prayed quietly, "Lord, I know you see us. Anything that would come against Mat'ta will have to go through me. You have given me headship over her as my wife; I submit her to you, Lord God, and declare your Lordship over us both. Anything that would come against me will have to go through You, Lord God. I submit myself to you. The battle is yours. The heavens and the earth belong to you, and now you hold all authority over everyone in them. You are my Defender. We trust you. We need you right now. I take my stand and resist Satan. Please command him to leave." He bent down low in a posture of humility, "we'll wait right here until you tell us it is time to move."

The Lord of Hosts, with his accompanying army, transported from the Serpent's Trees in the Oasis to the top of the cliff directly over the scene unfolding below Him. He was waiting for a certain sign. Noel stayed on his knees; I joined him at the cliff's edge and knelt next to him. I also bowed my head and closed my eyes. I could spiritually perceive the presence of the Serpent. I felt his challenge. Just as I determined in my heart to take his challenge and bind him, Noel took my hand in his and said, "we can wait, Lord. The battle is yours; we submit to your sovereignty and Lordship over us, and over our enemy." I received the warning from the Holy Spirit, held my tongue, and submitted to my husband's lead. Instantly, I felt a shield of protection fall over us. I knew we were untouchable. The striving in my spirit ceased. Something new moved into place; strength greater than power. I repeated Noel's words, "I submit to your sovereignty and Lordship over us and over our enemy." That was the sign The Lord of Hosts was waiting on: my submission to my husband's spiritual leadership, and Noel's determination to follow his spirit and not his logical thinking. The Holy Spirit enclosed Noel and Mat'ta within a shield of His presence. He had them securely in His care. The Lord of Hosts and his angelic guard moved from the ridge to the cave's edge, between Noel, Mat'ta, and the Serpent. Jesus spoke saying, "All authority is given unto me in heaven and in the earth." He had no need to use force with his voice or tone. Authority is far more potent than power.

The Serpent was impotent and it knew it was defeated. Satan lost all authority the day Jesus presented himself sinless and perfect as the slain Lamb of God. Satan gave up the keys of the Kingdom to Jesus on that day; the day the mystery of God burst into resurrection power. It was a decisive, judicial ruling from the throne of Heaven, an eternal and everlasting victory. The authority of the earth, forfeited by the first Adam, returned to Jesus upon His sacrificial death. Therefore, this Serpent had no personal authority on the earth. All it had was innate angelic size, the fear that accompanies intimidation, and the cunning deception that tricks believers into engaging in power struggles. Angelic power is no match for authority, ever.

Noel knows this truth, and used it in warfare, which is why he remained untouchable the entire time he roamed the Valley searching for Mat'ta. Repeatedly, throughout the year he lived in the desert, Noel came across victims of the Hunters. He used this weapon of warfare to protect and lead prodigals back to the Kingdom's Gate. The prodigals were humbling themselves; people were forsaking their pursuit of wickedness, and repenting of their rebellion. One heart at a time, God's people were returning home. The Serpent's power is no match for a truly repentant heart. Papa used Christ's authority to deliver all who called on His name. The Serpent had to play this smart: if it continued to challenge Jesus for the legal rights to Mat'ta,

Jesus could expel the Serpent from the territory. That defeat was far more serious than losing control of one prodigal. The expulsion was not a price it was willing to pay; therefore, it backed itself down the cliff face, and slithered away into the shadows of the desert floor; gone for now but not gone for good.

Chapter Four

THE SHIFTING

The Lord of Hosts gave his commands, "the shift is happening, their spirits are grasping the truth! All authority belongs to me! The great deception will end. My Bride will rise up! Prepare for war. Getting these two beloved humans back to the Kingdom is our first military mission. It is your responsibility to cooperate with the will of these Image-Bearers, but you are not to over step their will. Mat'ta is still very weak spiritually and unpredictable. Ultimately, she must choose humble submission. As she does, you are free to intervene for her good, Ma'oz. You are a faithful warrior, I trust you. Qayam and Gibbor, this battle belongs to me; I will win, with you at my side!"

Noel stood to his feet sensing the Holy Spirit urging him to get moving. He helped me to my feet as he said, "bring your spear, and any other weapons." He removed his outer shirt and handed it to me. "Here, Mat'ta. Put the ironwood seeds in this. Do you have anything to carry water?" I handed him the gourd flask I made when I was in the Oasis. "Good, this will work. It doesn't hold much, but it should get us through until we reach the Palace."

"Noel," I said as I started to launch into another apology, but he interrupted me.

"No, Mat'ta. I know we have to talk, but that will take longer than we have time for right now. Please, respect the fact that I need you to wait."

"But what if something happens to one of us? Things can't go left unsaid." I objected.

"And the four hundred nights that have passed between us since you walked out, was there not a real risk that things would go unsaid? It has waited this long; it will wait until we get home." Noel's words were strong but not harsh, and full of wisdom.

"Yes, you're right." I nodded my head. His logic cleared my shame. He was definitely right.

"I meant what I prayed, Mat'ta. Papa taught me that my safety is in the hidden place in Him. He truly is our Defender. He will protect us. We will make it home. Then we will talk... in the Garden." Noel finished what he was saying with a smile before he transitioned the topic. He put his hands on my shoulders, looked intently into my eyes and said, "If I tell you to run, I mean it. Run. Do not hesitate. You have been in this desert for a long time. You know the territory, but you are still broken, Beloved, and vulnerable to the Hunters. I have been in the wilderness nearly as long, but Papa taught me how to remain untouchable in this hellhole. I am not perfect, but I have a better chance of surviving an attack than you do. Use submission to Christ's authority as your defense. Remember, your greatest weapon is the Name of Jesus. If the yips of the Hunters overwhelm you, just keep saying the name of Jesus." He was right; I could not withstand an attack. "Say the name of Jesus... Say the name of Jesus," I reminded myself.

"Do we have everything?" he asked as he pointed toward the basket, "What about that rope?" He saw usefulness in everything; that is how his mechanical mind worked. I grabbed the rope and the basket. Who knows, maybe it would come in handy.

We climbed up to the ridge and walked among the shrubs and Desert Broom as far as the ridge carried us, but eventually it faded until it blended into the desert floor. Noel led until we hit the desert floor, then he instructed me to walk in front of him. Earlier, as we walked on the ridge, I looped the rope with the basket over my shoulder and under my armpit, leaving the basket dangling at my side. I placed the ironwood seeds and the gourd into the basket, and then tucked my spear between my shoulder blades with the spearhead above me. It rested snuggly against the small of my back, firmly between my skin and the rope. I held my slingshot in my left hand, a medium-sized rock in my right hand, ready to load it at any moment.

Noel had a short sword strapped to his right thigh. I am not sure how I missed it back in the cave; maybe he had laid it down outside the cave before approaching so I would not be frightened. Regardless, he had it now, and it gave me a sense of security. I took notice of the stark difference between us: He had his spiritual authority and its strength in tact and only one small weapon. I had a very weakened authority, and little faith, but several physical weapons. Clearly, we lived differently in this Valley, and only one of us lived well.

The day was waning and it would be dusk soon. Noel looked around for a place of safety. "Do you see that large mesquite tree about two hundred yards ahead of us?" Noel asked.

"Yes." I answered.

"We're going to climb it. Do you think you can do that?" He asked.

I nodded my head yes but my mind was saying, "I hope so."

"Okay, we need to be in the treetop by dark." We picked up a pace that was considerably faster, but still allowed for stealth and accuracy as we maneuvered along the desert floor.

The first stars were twinkling in the night sky when we reached the large mesquite tree. Noel removed my spear, and then helped me remove the rope harness. Without hesitating, he slung the basket up and over the thick bough of the tree and handed me the loose end. He then climbed the tree. "Now, hold on to the rope and I will hoist you up. If you can assist by pushing against the trunk, please do." Gibbor, his guardian, hovered just above Noel in the tree. When Noel began hoisting, Gibbor assisted. The task was easier than Noel anticipated, a sure sign he had help. "Thank you, Lord. Thank you for all you have done today. We cannot do any of this without you."

When I reached the first split in the tree boughs, Noel said, "Mat'ta, climb as high as you can. Stay to the thicker, sturdier branches closest to the trunk."

"Okay," I responded and then started climbing. Noel was literally right behind me in case I slipped or lost my balance. When we reached the last large bough, I tucked my back against the trunk and let my legs dangle to either side of the large branch. He asked me to scoot up to make room for him to slide in behind me. As he did, he wrapped the rope around us and the trunk, then secured it so that we could rest without risking a fall. We sat in silence for a few moments, but then Noel spoke in a soft whisper, "Mat'ta, I love you. I want you to know that has not changed in the slightest. I came to a point when I had to choose a path forward for my life. I chose us. We are worth the fight, and I will continue fighting until we get 'us' back." He kissed my cheek and pulled me in tight to his torso in a reassuring hug, and said, "right now, rest while I keep watch."

"I love you, Noel." I put my head back to rest on his shoulder. As I drifted off to sleep, my mind turned to the children and I heard echoes of their voices. "Thank you, Papa." In the safety of Noel's arms, I let my mind drift. Could it be that my own warfare opened me up to suffering? I definitely rebuked the Serpent, repeatedly and harshly, over this past year or better. I definitely entered his territory with the intention of picking a fight. Papa did not lead me into war; I chose it, as my revenge. The book of Jude came to mind as clear as if I was reading it from the Bible. Did I leave my own abode and engage the enemy in his territory? It seemed possible, if not likely. I was accountable before God for my entire past year. Papa and I had a lot to talk through, and it would start with repentance… I was asleep before the sentence was finished.

Noel spoke to Jesus in his mind, "Lord, thank you for keeping Mat'ta alive. She is in a desperate state, Lord. She is broken and weak; a shadow of the woman I have loved for years. Her apathy and lack of spiritual awareness is frightening. I cannot get her home by my own effort. Her spiritual dullness will attract the hordes of Hunters between here and the Gates. I need you to come get us. I know you see us. Come get us, Lord." Off in the distance, Noel could hear the yipping of the Hunters. "Mat'ta, get ready." I jumped in a startle at the sound of Noel's voice. For just a moment, I forgot I was with him being unaccustomed to his presence. "I'm awake," I said as I straightened my posture, "did you hear something?" Noel answered, "the Hunters are near. They are going to find us. They will not be able to reach us, but that will not stop their relentless yipping. You have to fight for your own life, Mat'ta. I am not your Savior. You know the Savior, call on His name." In the treetop, hovering above Noel and Mat'ta, the angelic guardians stood prepared for the expected onslaught. They knew Mat'ta's choices in this exact battle determined the course of her future.

Just as Noel drew his short sword from the sheath on his thigh, the Alpha Hunter arrived at the base of the mesquite tree. It hooked its large claws into the side of the tree and pulled upward. General Qayam took to flight with his sword drawn, diving directly at the Alpha Hunter. In one accurate swipe, he sliced the hindquarter of its right leg. The Hunter instantly buckled under its own weight and tumbled to the side. Noel took note of the injury. Though the strike was invisible in the physical realm, Noel knew Papa had heard his prayer and answered it. The angelic warriors were present and they had entered the battle. The Alpha Hunter began its evil serenade of yipping, and all I could hear were the accusations I had spoken against God with their intentional disdain. I put my hands over my ears, as I had done so many nights in the past, but this time I did as Noel had said; I took a stand. "I repent. I choose you, Jesus. You are for me, not against me. Even in my rebellion, you came for me. I belong to you. I am not my own. You paid the full price for me. You died because of me! You died for me! You died as me! You rose from the grave alive! You are the perfect Lamb of God, slain for the sins of the world! You have all authority over your enemies. I submit to you, Lord. I lay my life before you. I stop my self-defense, right now, right here. There is no one like you.

There is no Savior but you. I put my trust in you, Jesus, King of Kings, Lord of Lords, Mighty God, and Prince of Peace..." As I continued exalting the names of God, the Alpha's yipping became yelps. God's great name, and the spiritual authority it carries, tortured the unclean spirit. Its yipping accusations stopped completely in the presence of authentic, sincere praise. I did not have to scream or yell to be effective, but I chose to do so. New strength surged into my spirit as I rehearsed the truth of the Word. When I stopped my yelling, I realized the Hunter was gone. I also realized I was in the tree alone. Noel had climbed out of the tree to take his stand with his own strong declarations of truth.

In the invisible realm, Qayam, Gibbor, Etsem, and Ma'oz shouted in synchronized victory cries. Their angelic bodies illuminated the heavenlies for miles, displacing the darkness and chasing away the shadows of evil. Our human spirits filled with holy light as well, and we became the light on a hill Jesus spoke of: a lighthouse on the rocky shores of a coastline. Other prodigals lost in the Serpent's Valley sensed the holy presence of God and turned their eyes toward the palace wall. The trajectory of the future changed. Everyone, human or angelic knew it was time to head to the Gate.

Chapter Five

RUN HOME, MAT'TA

"Mat'ta, climb down quickly," Noel commanded with a strong urgency while he scoured the desert, looking for movement. I obeyed immediately. When I reached the bottom limb, I dropped my legs over one side, balanced on my torso until I had a good grip with my hands, then I dangled my body before I dropped the remainder of the distance to the ground. "We have to move our location. You are going to run for your life, Mat'ta. I am going to fight for you. Do not look back, just run, right now!"

I am the Hunted. I know it. The victory in the tree was just the beginning. "Jesus... Jesus" I did what I was told and repeated my Defender's name. Something began growling, just off in the distance. It was probably another Hunter or maybe the same Hunter; regardless, the growling tells me I am the target. My instinct told me to run, but I did not want to leave Noel, and for a moment, I considered defying his instructions. As I hesitated, Noel took off in a dead run in the direction of more growling. It was too late. I was already alone. Run. Pant. I rest briefly. Listen. Get my bearings. Then run again. It was inevitable. I knew this very moment would come at some point. Thoughts of Papa's warnings to guard my mind, and His pleas for me to spend time with Him so that He could strengthen my spirit, all rushed through my mind like flood waters. Why did I resist Him? Why did I demand my own way? Why did... "I don't know. I don't know!" I say to myself, shaking my head, as if I could shake off regret. I stopped and stood still, holding my breath so that I could hear everything around me. "Focus, Mat'ta." I whispered, but in my mind, I scolded myself for the ill-timed introspection. Up ahead of me, the moonlight outlined the wall that surrounds the Kingdom Palace. Breaching the wall looked manageable from this distance, as if I can scale it with a good run at it, but I know better. When I am standing at the wall, it will tower above me... three or four stories high. The only way in is through the Gate, so I must navigate this wilderness with the Gate as my destination.

Holy Spirit hovered over me, speaking words I would recognize from my childhood. "Beloved, there will come a day when you need me. Just call on my name!" The words bounced off the walls of my mind as an echo. "Just call on my name! Just call on my name!" Of all the words Papa spoke over me, it is no coincidence that I recall these specific words in this very moment, as I run from the Hunter. "Papa God, Lord Jesus! Help me!" Instinct, or maybe panic, pushed my thoughts forward. I felt my body fill with adrenaline and a compulsion to run on. Is that not what prey always does, runs in panic? I forced myself to wait out the moment. Just as I began to step forward, I felt strong arms fold around me. I knew this Presence. The Holy Spirit held me, and said, "Beloved. Stop. Be still. I am with you. I will help you." I stopped and stooped behind a fallen tree. I listened. The Hunter was close. "Please save me." I pleaded with the Holy Spirit. I felt an instant calmness rush into my mind.

With my cry for help, Ma'oz filled with radiant light. His might was not his own, it was Papa's might. Ma'oz unfurled his wings, and nudged me forward. Holy Spirit swirled around me forming cords of restraint, called Love and Goodness. I could feel the restraints clasp around my torso. Papa trained me as a young child to trust these cords and accept them as intuition and discernment. I instantly felt infused with courage and hope. I was going to escape the grasp of this Hunter. I would find my way to the Gate.

I clearly heard the voice of God in my mind, "Come along quickly, Mat'ta. Do not be frightened. Do not look around anxiously." Holy Spirit led me by His cords, and I responded by trusting my intuition. Ma'oz guarded me from behind as we moved through the Desert Broom and cactus. We moved in a weaving pattern to confuse the Hunter that was tracking us. Ma'oz was using his wings as a shield, reflecting the desert back onto itself; the Hunter struggled to get any good confirmation of our location. Even though heaven was helping me, I had to get into a mindset of trust; I started repeating the name of Jesus, "Jesus... Jesus... Jesus..." It stunned me how His great name stopped the panic that was causing my confusion. "Jesus you are so good... you are so good. You warned me, Papa. You warned me about the Hunters and the real danger in the Serpent's Valley. Why didn't I listen?" It was more of a statement than a question. Holy Spirit swirled around my body in an upward spiral. I felt the immediate lift in my spirit and redirected my words, "you are so patient with me and so kind. Somehow, you will make good out of this season of my life. I do not know if the sifting is over, Papa, but blame shifting ends now. It is time to face my own evil."

Yips of the Hunter translated in my mind as a question rising between us, "why would he take you back just because of a simple prayer? You spent the last year accusing Him of murdering your children. What happened to your right to wander? Why did you go into the territory of the Hunter?"

Shame rose with a heat in my face until my ears burned and turned red.

Holy Spirit moved over me. I could feel His person and hear Him say, "Beloved, shame is not becoming of you. Do not settle for shame. Let Sorrow attend to your soul. She will lead you into healing found in repentance. Follow her."

Ma'oz guided and nudged me to the edge of a wide, dry riverbed. In rainy seasons, it filled with rushing run-off water from the mountains, but most of the year it was dry and sandy. Over the years, along the bend in the river, rushing water forged deep crevices in the banks that looked like shallow caves. About a six-foot drop directly below us was one of these caves. I leapt into the riverbed; Ma'oz broke my fall so that I landed without injury. Though I could not see him, I could sense his protection as he gently shoved me against the dirt wall. The Hunter caught up to me. It was just above me on the ledge, crouched on its belly like a spring about to release. His head and nose hung over the edge, eyes narrowed and focused. Hunter vs. Hunted. It began signaling to the pack. I could hear the other pack members yipping. I could feel the evil rushing toward me. Then suddenly, the dust of the riverbed began to whip around me with such force, it barricaded the Hunters. I guarded my face from the swirling sand as it began rising over my head, creating a pillar of cloud so thick, nothing could penetrate it. The Hunter's yips and growls, along with the incessant fear from evil's close proximity, all grew silent by the rushing swirls of Sorrow's Whirlwind. As the Tempest of God whipped into a massive funnel, it became my fortress. Evil could no longer reach me. I could not see Holy Spirit or Ma'oz, but I sensed they were with me. Relief flooded my body. I was perfectly safe in the eye of the Tempest, able to breathe and think again. As the funnel widened, it gave me more territory as protection. I stood up from my stoop against the dirt wall and calmly walked into the open space created by the Tempest.

"Holy Spirit, this is amazing!" I said as I turned slowly in circles to observe the 360 degrees of manifest peace around me. His presence was so tangible; I felt His mercy fall over me as drops of oil, like a gentle, living rain. He, Himself, anointed me with His mercy. I turned my face up to the heavenly drops as each one mixed with the thick layer of dust on my skin. I could smell the wilderness on me mixed with the fragrant oil of gladness. I stood with my face to the sky as it washed my hair from my forehead. "The Rain of Sorrow," I said to myself. Once drenched in heavenly drops of mercy, something awakened inside me as if my heart and mind were coming out of a long coma. I did not resist the flood of truth set free from the prison of my will: After I lost Elizabeth, I steeled my emotions with indifference; I stopped grief with accusation. I stopped guilt for abandoning Noel with the thought that he is better off without me. I intentionally lived every day on the edge of danger; adrenaline replaced feeling grief. I became accustomed to this counterfeit life and its false sense of purpose for survival. Exhaustion overwhelmed my body; I felt old. I felt worn down. When was the last time I let real rest tempt my mind? I cannot recall when I slept deeply enough to dream; at least not until I dreamt of the children. Since that dream of my children, all I have done is weep. My soul was so full of grief and anger, it made crying involuntary, almost intrusive and I could not stop; as if my spirit demanded a voice, and my sobs spoke a language I do not speak. The harder I cried, the harder it rained down mercy.

Odunay, Papa's name for His angelic minister of Sorrow, appeared before me. She held in her hand a beautiful, ornate jar of anointing oil. Odunay has attended me before. She always comes with pure compassionate comfort. Her strength is in her silence. Her intimacy with Papa overflowed from her heart and deeply ministered to me. She was not compelled to say anything at all; she simply knelt beside me and sang over me. Her voice poured over my soul like a concerto as she spoke my story through her spiritual song of rich, deep tones that strummed the chords of my spirit. I could not understand her words because she sang in a heavenly language, but I felt their purpose. Papa's intentions for my life and his compassionate love saturated my innermost being, bypassing my rebellious mind, so that I would not reject his lovingkindness. He had a full measure of mercy in mind for me; a measure so full I would deem myself unworthy of it if I comprehended it. That is the wisdom of a prayer language. Odunay combed her fingers through my wet hair, her own hands fragrant with the oil of gladness. As she sang, she worked to form an intricate braid of my unkempt hair. Her touch was as soothing as her song. "Mat'ta, there is an ancient truth most humans reject, but it is the truth you seek."

"What is that truth, Odunay?" I asked with genuine curiosity.

"Sorrow is better than laughter: the sorrow you hold in your spirit is necessary for the discipline of the Lord to complete its work of purging. Sorrow leads you into the house of mourning where wisdom trains your spirit to rule over your soul. So many believers never complete this stage, and their lives get shipwrecked on the shores of offense." I rebutted, "I don't understand, Odunay. What good can come from mourning?" My question exposed that I remained stranded on these shores of offense myself. Odunay continued, "Sorrow purifies the treasury vault of the soul. Your flesh is intolerant of suffering; it rebels like a misbehaving child who demands its own way; and in doing so, it reveals the wickedness it keeps for use in times of suffering. Gladness and prosperity do not cause your soul to reveal its arsenal. Only suffering completes this work." As Odunay spoke, she picked up two broken pieces of a Saguaro rib from the floor of the riverbed, twisted the braid onto the top of my head, and secured it with the broken ribs. "Mat'ta, you tumbled into love with Jesus; you lived a carefree and vibrant life. You danced when new truth exploded into your understanding, you sang with your whole body, you could not help but share your love affair with Jesus with as many people as would listen, and many did listen, Mat'ta." I agreed, "Yes, it is my favorite time of my life. I lived lost in Jesus; some days would pass so quickly; it was as if I had actually been swept away to somewhere else." Even as I spoke of this time in my life, my heart filled with hope and longing.

"And do you remember what Jesus asked of you?" Odunay probed gently.

"Yes, He asked to be King of my heart and the lover of my soul." I answered.

"What was your answer to His proposal?" she asked.

"I said yes, wholeheartedly." I answered.

"How did you seal your covenant promise?" It was a question, but it hit my spirit as a declaration.

"With a cup..." my voice trailed off in the middle of my answer as the realization hit my conscious mind, "with a cup of suffering." Odunay agreed with my answer, "yes, He sealed your covenant with a cup of suffering, just as Jesus offered His closest friends around the table of His last meal. You are a beloved disciple, Mat'ta. You cried out with desperation to know Jesus more. Do you remember the ache you felt from longing in your heart for something more? Do you remember how meaningless life felt to you? 'There has to be more to knowing Him than just reading about His life in a book.' Those were your words; the words that compelled Him to woo you into the Wilderness so that He could prepare you for deeper spiritual life."

I interjected, "wait. Before this moment, it has not crossed my mind that Papa played a part in my running away into the Valley of the Serpent. I always believed that decision was my desire for independence." Odunay explained, "It was your desire for independence that led you to the Valley, specifically. He would have gone in any direction, Mat'ta, regardless of where you ran. You chose the Valley of the Serpent. You chose the place of purging. He warned you of its dangers, but it did not deter Him from His mission. He was with you at all times." I spoke more to myself than I did to Odunay when I responded, "it was my strong will… it was my selfishness… it was my put-me-above-others way of living that needed to be purged…" It was beginning to make sense. Suffering is Papa's passage into deeper spiritual life. It is not random and meaningless. Suffering filleted open my innermost being and exposed how I aligned my own choices with darkness, how I personally became hostile against God. "When my hidden evil came into the light, all those times I accused Papa, I had the opportunity to crucify my flesh." Odunay nodded in agreement as she continued, "'pick up your cross and follow me' was the invitation Jesus gave you to the 'more' of life. The willing, full submission of your soul to Him is much deeper than simply obeying Papa's rules. He is not interested in settling for an external relationship built on obligation as its foundation. Obedience to righteousness is required in His Kingdom, but it flows most easily from a will that bends in submission because it has been conquered by His goodness." We both sat silent for a moment while I contemplated the truth in what she was saying. Even in the state of spiritual dullness, I remembered the clarity of discernment I had when Holy Spirit wooed me to choose life through repentance. He repeatedly offered me a way of escape out of suffering; I repeatedly offered pretentious arguments and excuses that defended my flesh. Then Odunay asked, "can you drink the cup He drinks? He emptied the covenant cup and accepted the will of His Father above his own. Can you do the same?" I answered, "I agreed to, but I did not know the price of suffering would harden my heart toward Papa; how hostile I would become." She interrupted, "He did. He knew. This is why He submitted His own will to the will of His Father in the Garden, to prepare the way for you. Your sights are on the Gate of the Kingdom, but He waits for you in the Garden of Mourning."

Odunay finished her work and turned me toward a small puddle of the heavenly drops, which had formed near my knees. It reflected the sun as a mirror. She encouraged me to look at my reflection in the pool of mercy. "See Beloved," Sorrow whispered as she leaned over my shoulder, "beauty for ashes. You now wear the crown of Beauty, Child of God, chosen and favored one. Papa loves you without measure. He sees the spirit of heaviness within you. You have broken places He will heal. He will anoint you, heal you, and break you free." Then Odunay spoke more pointedly, "what is true in your life is not necessarily The Truth. When you separate the two, you will be on your way to healing." With that striking thought, Odunay, Tempest of God, lifted high above me. The drops of heaven stopped. When the Tempest Cloud lifted, I was no longer in the Valley of the Serpent. I stood on the outskirt boundaries of the Garden of Mourning.

Chapter Six

THE GARDEN

Checed and Tob, Papa's angelic ministers of Goodness and Mercy, stood on the rise of the rolling hills. Both angelic beings were of formidable size, dressed in white linen garments gathered at the waist with a golden belt. Their garments moved as if they were weightless and floating on a breeze. Flames danced around their heads, and stood suspended above their hands as they reached out to greet me. Fear flooded my mind, but the Presence of the Holy Spirit was so strong, I knew intuitively these servants of God were safe and that they knew me intimately; and somehow, I knew them as faithful friends, though it was the first time my eyes had seen them.

"Mat'ta, 'Planting of the Lord'," the angels spoke my name with its full meaning, "do not be afraid. Come with us, Beloved. Jesus has prepared the table, and He waits expectantly for you."

As I climbed the rise to join my hosts, I looked out over the valley below. Sheep were grazing casually in the vast meadows, near calm streams of water. The hills were full of wild flowers, especially lilies and tulips that danced a synchronized dance with the willow trees in the gentle breeze. The sun was warm on my skin, but not harsh as it was in the Valley of the Serpent. As I took in a restorative breath, I picked up the fragrance of the Lord's anointing: aloe, cassia, and myrrh. The Lord is here; not only Jesus, but Papa, too, who was already running in my direction with His regal robe flying in the wind behind Him. I broke into a full run as I yelled out, "Papa, I'm here!" Without breaking His stride, He picked me up, swung me around, and laughed with pure pleasure. "Mat'ta, my Beloved!" He said as He kissed my forehead, my eyes, and my cheeks repeatedly, just as He did when I was a young child. Papa, God of the Universe, was celebrating my return as if it was all that mattered to Him in the whole universe. He did not withhold His heart or affection from me; instead, He poured out His love with such abandon it raptured me and caught me up into His reality, where there is no condemnation.

When he put me back on my feet, His majesty stunned my senses. How beautiful He is, dressed in his finest robe of every color; the robe with the names of God stitched in gold throughout. One name blended into the next, each identifiable, but mysteriously appearing to shape the outline of "I AM." His crown of such pure gold shone like crystal and rested on his head as if it were part of Him. His breastplate of twelve stones covered His broad chest; held in place by His magnificent belt called Truth, so intricate in detail, it rightly reflected His splendor, His glory, and identified His Kingdom authority. His Sword was present, but in its sheath on His right thigh. Every step He took left a footprint, lit up with glory, and the written word 'peace' in the soil. He is the KING of Kings, the Great I Am. The wonder of His beauty raptured all of creation into reverent worship. I could not help but praise Him, no matter my personal condition. His majestic presence commanded worship because He is so utterly worthy of it. His angels, Checed and Tob, filled with Papa's glory and transformed from physical beings back into spirit, but I could only see indistinguishable swirls of light. Ma'oz joined them, and transformed into his natural, created form. They sang in heavenly languages as they danced for Papa, until pure pleasure poured out of Papa in joyful laughing. In all my days, I have never felt more liberated than I did in that worship. Then, Papa whispered to still our worship. I felt the touch of a strong hand on my arm. Jesus stood before me with a smile on his face and his arms stretched out as an invitation for a sincere embrace. Without hesitation, I wrapped my arms around his head as he wrapped his arms around my waist. Being in His arms was as if I had come home. We both giggled with such delight, the angels joined in. Heavenly laughter was everywhere. As he swung me around in circles, I felt as if I was riding waves of joy. He was glad to see me. My fears of rejection had been unwarranted.

"Mat'ta, we have so much to talk about… so much to do… but nothing is more pressing than welcoming you home." Mercy poured out of the abundance of His love; with mercy, I could feel the fruit of sorrow rising to the surface. Repentance without regret or restraint poured out of my spirit. "I'm a rebel, Jesus, a prodigal." Saying this truth aloud cleared the fog that had attended my soul for more than a year. My heart poured out all I had done and why I felt compelled to do so; I had grown so defiant against Papa; so obstinate with my stiff-armed resistance against His pursuit of me because I wanted to protect my right to independence, my right to rule over my own life. "It is all pride, isn't it, Lord? I led myself into my own destruction." Sorrow filled my heart. Not shame, not condemnation. Honest, sincere sorrow flooded my soul.

Papa joined Jesus and me. Turning to Him, I said, "Papa, I have been your enemy. Still you rescued me. I do not know how you made it so real, but… seeing each child… looking them in the eye... hearing their giggles... being a part of their joy... for that moment in time, I felt ... whole. You found me, Papa, where I lost me."

"Mat'ta, I know how deep your sorrow and grief plunged you into despair. What you could not see through your pain was the perfecting work of your suffering." As He spoke those words, He waved His hand over His head as the angels parted to make a way for us. We walked for a moment in silence until we came to an altar, one much like the altar Abraham placed Isaac upon in the Wilderness. "I have prepared a table before you in the presence of your enemies." He had not said so, but I knew, somehow, Papa would ask me to place what I held most dear on that altar: my children and my husband; they are the obvious sacrifice needed, but my intuition told me there was something more. Once this "something more" was sacrificed, my enemies would lose their hold over me.

"I did what I am asking of you. I sacrificed my only Son. Jesus willingly laid down His life to satisfy my greater will. Will you do the same?" He handed me the goblet of wine He had prepared for me. "The cup of Suffering," He said as I took it from His hand. I drank it until it was empty. I determined to do whatever was required of me. Next, I anticipated His discipline and exposure, but I received a miracle.

Papa stepped to the side so that I could gaze over the altar. Jesus was dancing and playing with Rachel, Michael, and the rest of my children. They turned to me and waved. Papa laughed with hearty pleasure and blew them each a kiss; one by one, they pretended to catch it in mid-air, fell to the ground from the weight of it, and rolled among the lilies. Jesus caught his own kiss from his Father and joined the children in their pretend play. Unadulterated joy; there was no other way to describe it. The children each sat up in the grass, as Michael yelled, "we love you, Mama!"

Papa stepped back in front of me and blocked my view of the children. "You see, Mat'ta, I have kept them in perfect peace. The evil of the world has never touched them, and you will be with them in eternity. For a short time, I have separated them from you. The loss of your children became the anvil of perfection. Your flesh, as all flesh does, fought against suffering. Under suffering's divine pressure, you wholeheartedly pursued what is contrary to your spirit. You chose abandonment. Without suffering, abandonment remained a hidden palace where you sit on the throne, ruling your own life separate from me; it has always been a stronghold within you. Because of suffering, you ran deep into the dark kingdom, straight to this hidden palace within your soul, and eventually took up residence in a cave among my enemies.

Where can you hide that I cannot find you? Whom did I send to rescue you, Mat'ta?" I answered, "The Spirit of God... my amazing husband... my perfect children... your faithful angelic warriors..." Papa nodded his head in agreement as compassion spread across His face. "I never lost you, Mat'ta. I never left you. I was with you in the cave. I was with you in the desert. I was with you at the Oasis. And when suffering had completed its work, I rescued you." Papa stepped to the side once again and I saw Noel completely enveloped by our children. I do not know when he arrived in the Garden, or if angels escorted him here, but my heart was thrilled and relieved to see he was safely delivered from the Valley of the Serpent. I stepped closer to the altar so that I could witness the healing of Noel's reunion, just as I experienced in the cave.

I watched with sincere empathy and understanding as he spoke softly to Rachel. I could not hear his words, but I knew he was pouring out his love for her, expressing the dreams he carried in his heart. Every word spoken was full of life, of this, I was certain. She looked into her Daddy's eyes with adoration and respect, nodding her head in agreement with his words. When he finished, he embraced her in a long embrace, kissing her forehead as she leaned into his chest.

Michael intruded on Rachel and hugged his Dad with

pounding slaps to the middle of his back, just as men often do when they hug each other. When Noel reached up to ruffle his full head of hair, Michael ducked away in a teasing manner to avoid the ruffle then turned and ran away. Noel was in immediate pursuit until he overcame Michael and tackled him to the ground. The two rolled around in the meadow as they laughed with one another. They both rolled to their stomachs as Noel spoke his love and aspirations for Michael. They stayed in that position for some time as they talked until Michael rolled to his back and began tossing a stone he found in the grass above his head, catching it mere inches from his eyes. Repeatedly, he tossed the stone while their conversation continued. When it was over, Noel stood to his feet and offered his hand to pull Michael to his feet, straight into a final, sincere embrace. Michael wrapped his arms around his Father's head and buried his own head against Noel's neck, man to man.

Thomas and Tasha wedged themselves between the two men, and wrapped their arms around Noel's thighs. Michael stepped back and kissed the top of each head as Noel bent down and lifted them into each arm. He alternated kissing the cheek of each toddler, as they squealed in delight, "again, Daddy." The kisses continued until Noel bent down to sit on the ground. Thomas and Tasha took turns sitting in his lap as they showed him flowers, bugs, and rocks. He showed interest in everything they told him as if he had never seen a flower, bug, or a rock before this very moment.

"That is a beautiful picture of a Father's love, Mat'ta, would you not agree?" My heart was already swelling with pride and adoration for the man before me. "I have loved him almost my entire life, Papa; he loves me just as purely as you see him loving his sweet babies right now."

"Yes, indeed Mat'ta, he was fashioned specifically for you. I am very proud of him. He has become a giant of a man, a man after my own heart. He has proven to be quite trustworthy and pure of heart. The angels have gone to referring to him as Braveheart. I think it's very fitting; what do you think?"

"Absolutely," I said wholeheartedly in agreement.

Peter, John-Mark, and Timothy joined Noel and the toddlers as they wrestled with each other in the grass nearby. Noel engaged them immediately, tackling two at a time, with the third mounting his back. As young boys do, they each took turns challenging Noel in tests of strength: arm wrestling, leg wrestling, and tackling. Noel did not immediately give in to their efforts to topple him; wisdom naturally led him to meet their challenge and beat them at their game to encourage a heartier effort. Before the war games were over, all four males were dripping with sweat, but something amazing had happened: respect and honor birthed within the hearts of these young men. They admired their Father and it was clear they longed to be like him. "The love of a Father is so vital for a child, Papa. Look at how they admire him," I said with my own admiration. All of the wrestling had landed the heap of men at the edge of the stream. Peter leaned over to cup some water in his hands to drink; just as his hand reached his mouth, Noel playfully shoved him into the water, which broke into a full-fledged water fight with kicking and spitting fountains.

"Is that water sanitary, Papa?"

Papa laughed a full belly laugh, "does it matter at this point?"

Rachel approached the group, carrying a sleeping baby. Rachel swaddled Elizabeth to help her feel secure; she slept more soundly wrapped tightly and at this time of day, nothing would disturb her slumber. When Noel noticed Rachel's approach, he got out of the water and walked toward her. "He did not know about Elizabeth, Papa. I never told him I was pregnant because I knew I was leaving him." Rachel gave Elizabeth to her Daddy. As Noel took the baby from Rachel's arms, he looked over at me. Even with the distance between us, I could read his body language; everything about him said, "Why didn't you tell me?" Noel dropped to his knees with Elizabeth to his chest. He bent over her and wept. "Why does he cry, Mat'ta?" The question hung in the air, not because Papa did not know the answer, but because He wanted me to face the answer. "He cries because he has not grieved her yet." I answered Papa. The other seven children gathered around him as he grieved. They all remained huddled for quite some time. It was difficult to distinguish between one from the other. Papa said, "go join them, Mat'ta. It's time to say goodbye."

I ran into the field and fell to my knees when I reached the huddle. Noel opened his left arm to me as an invitation to join him. I took Elizabeth from him and snuggled her close to my face. The smell of her skin and her hair filled my heart. The other children maneuvered themselves in front of us, except for the twins, who sat in Noel's lap. "Your mother and I dreamt of you, each one of you, from the very start of our marriage. We grew up together, literally. We were your ages when we fell in love" pointing to Rachel and Michael, "and we have faced life side by side. Your lives are rich and full, kids. You never walked on earth, like other children, but you have fulfilled a deep and lasting purpose. The pain of losing you was in the exact measure needed for Papa to forge our character. We are the people we are today because we have you; and we will become the people He intends for us to become because we lost you. We will wholeheartedly tell your story. With Papa's grace and blessing, maybe others will come to understand the beautiful purpose of children like you."

Elizabeth woke as Noel concluded, and the first thing she said was, "Mama." I said through a smile, "yes, sweet baby girl, it's Mama. And this is your Daddy." Elizabeth squirmed to break free of the swaddle, so I loosened it; as I did, she reached her chubby fingers to her Daddy's face to touch his beard. Noel took her from my arms and held her tight again. All was right with the world.

Papa stood with us, and spoke very tenderly. "It's time to say goodbye." Michael spoke up first, "it won't be long, and we'll see you soon. Of course, that's easy for me to say since I live with no time." Peter shoved Michael, but we all giggled at his attempt at humor. Rachel took the baby from Noel's arms and held Tasha's hand, "we love you, Mama. We love you, Daddy." She said with a bright smile as she stood to her feet and turned to follow Jesus. We all followed her lead and stood to our feet. The three older boys and Thomas hugged their Dad and got in one last playful punch as they ran away to catch Rachel and the girls. Thomas was last of the group of boys to turn away. He snuck in one last squeeze around our knees as Noel ruffled his hair. "We love you, son," we said in unison as he ran to catch the others. Michael was the last one standing. "Most kids who live where we live never get to meet their parents. I do not know why that is, but I am deeply grateful Papa granted us this gift. I am proud to be your son. We may never see each other again on earth, but we will be waiting for you." He hugged us both at the same time, pulling us together into one group hug. He turned to run and catch the others but yelled over his shoulder, "I love you!"

Noel turned to me and smiled.

"You knew this was going to happen, didn't you?" I said teasingly.

"No, I just knew we would meet in the Garden… and we would talk."

He took my hand as we walked with Papa back to the altar of stones.

"Thank you, Papa, for such an amazing gift. You have healed so much of my pain as we have met together in the secret place over these years; but this… this is beyond all I could have hoped or imagined. Eternity will be glorious." Noel looked back over his shoulder one last time in the direction of the children, just as their silhouettes dropped below the horizon.

"Braveheart, it is my greatest pleasure to give you the desires of your heart. I am so pleased with you. Your suffering has transformed you into a man I can trust. Your obedience urges me to bless you with more; more authority, more power, more opportunity, and I will do so; but in this moment, I ask you this: what if I never intend for you to make an impact and leave your mark in the earth? What if you never possess what you see others possessing? What if your life is summed up in one accomplishment: raising the next Elijah and Elisha for the coming days?"

Noel felt the gravity of the questions in his spirit. Does this mean he must sacrifice his innate desire to leave a lasting legacy? The implications of that reality contradicted his temperament and commitment to excellence. What does that look like? Questions rolled over his mind, one after another. He did not have enough detail to process the questions, but if Papa asked something of him, he had one answer: "Your will be done, Lord. That settles that right now. Whatever happens next, regardless of what it requires, we will work through it together. Besides, Papa, my enemies hold nothing in their hands that is worth holding on to if it means distance between you and me.

Papa gently moved me until I stood in front of Noel. Noel and I both looked at Papa with confusion at first, then resolution. Noel took both of my hands in his own and said to me, "Mat'ta, you are the love of my life, no matter what that life might look like, you hold my heart. When you left me, you shattered my heart. For a while I had to think to breathe, I hurt so badly; but eventually, Holy Spirit helped me pick up the shattered pieces. I carried the fragments of my broken heart into the Divine Court, and presented my case before God. Together, Papa and I rearranged the priorities of my life. It was not easy to wrestle my soul into submission; in fact, at times it felt torturous, but in the end, Papa restored my soul." Noel took in a deep breath and closed his eyes for a moment. When he opened them, Gibbor, his guardian angel, in obedience to Papa, placed an ornate box on the altar. Noel took note of it, but continued his thought and intention before he focused on the box. "Mat'ta, I put you in Papa's hands. I choose you, and I would search the world over for you again if need be, but you can no longer sit on the throne of my heart. I willfully remove you, but I put you in the care of the one I love most. I know He treasures you more than I do."

"Thank you, Braveheart, for this honor. Your sincere commitment and selfless love for Mat'ta makes your sacrifice priceless," Papa said as He acknowledged Noel's dedication at the altar.

"Now, Braveheart, examine what is placed on the altar."

Noel reached over the altar's edge and opened the ornate box. Inside were the shattered pieces he had presented in the Divine Court. All the hurt and offense he once felt because of my abandonment were contained in those fragments; as well as the grief he had over the loss of each of our children. Now, he knew something else was among the fragments: all the aspirations he once held for his own legacy, and how he wanted to be remembered by others; all of his works for God, constructed with precision and excellence, which carried a sense of definition of his person; and lastly, his future plans for his own life. The gravity he felt when Papa first presented His questions now made sense to him. "This is my sacrifice on the altar of suffering, Papa. I give you all of what I hold most dear, all that defines me; and most of all, my future. Not my will, but your will be done, Father." Checed and Tob, the angelic ministers of goodness and mercy, each leaned over the altar and ignited the box with the flames suspended from their hands. As the box caught fire, flames lifted an aroma so richly familiar it was unmistakably the aroma of Noel's life laid down.

Papa offered Noel a cup and bread. Together, they remembered Christ's sacrifice as Noel received communion. Their words were private, spoken only between them. When they were complete, Noel embraced Papa, and Papa reciprocated the embrace as He whispered in His ear, "I am so pleased with you, Son. For now, Goodness and Mercy will attend to you in our secret place. Go with them; I will be along soon. Right now, Mat'ta and I have things to discuss."

Okay, Papa," he said and he began to walk in the same direction the children had walked, Tob and Checed flanked him on either side as pillars of holy flame. "Take care of my best girl, Papa." He waved and blew me a kiss, "I love you, Mat'ta, more than ever!"

Chapter Seven

NEW BEGINNINGS

"The treasure of my heart just walked over the edge of the horizon, Papa." I said, knowing that every child represented my offering on the altar. Even though my family lived in perfect peace, safely in the care of my God, separation from them made me feel hollow.

"Mat'ta, the treasure of your heart stands with you now." He said.

"Yes, Papa, I know, but…" There it was, the 'something more.' It rolled out of my mouth before I could catch it and keep it hidden. The truth: Papa was not my treasure. When did that happen?

He knew my thoughts. There was no condemnation, just truth.

"Shall we see what is truly held as the treasure of your heart, Child?"

"Yes, please, Papa." He has always known, but the revelation that He is not my first affection shocked my conscience. "If I am blind to this truth, what other deception am I embracing? There is most definitely something, because abandoning those I treasure was my first response to suffering."

"Where did you run to and to whom?"

"I ran to the Plains of Carnal Pleasure, or at least that was my intent. I was running home. I was returning to a people who were like me, to find the orphans..."

"Mat'ta, do you remember what Jesus said to Thomas when He was telling the disciples He was going away to prepare a place for them, and that He would return for them?

"I think so. He said He is the way, the truth, and the life. No one gets to the Father except through Him."

"Yes, Mat'ta, and what was the destination?" Papa asked. I thought for a moment. It was not what, but who; Papa is the destination, and there is only one path. In one short exchange of words, everything about my misdirected life was exposed. I did not see Papa as my destination or my treasure. Clearly, I am my own treasure, and carnal pleasure is my destination.

"What did you think you would find when you arrived?"

"Acceptance… equality… I thought I would be free to do as I pleased, to live without consequence… well, at least without judgment. I wanted to live by my own standard of righteousness since I seemed to fall so short of yours." My heart poured out all of my intentions to taste the ways of the world, forgetting the ways of the Kingdom. I had grown so defiantly resistant to His pursuit of me. "I wanted to protect my right to independence; my right to rule over my own life."

"Mat'ta, let's walk a bit." Papa took my hand in His and turned back toward the hill from which I originally arrived in the Garden of Mourning. As we came to the crest of the hill, we could see a vast shoreline. Tob and Checed, Papa's angelic ministers, had my full attention when I first arrived at the Garden of Mourning, so I did not look behind me; I was unaware of the shoreline that now stretched out in front of me.

On the shoreline, I could see the waves swirl into funnels and then collapse again as Holy Spirit played in the waves. Jesus waded into the water waist deep as He yelled, "Encore! Encore!"

"You, the Triune God, are continually joyful! I love how you play! You make me want to let go and just live life like a kid. I want to be like you!" I yelled as I ran down the hill to the shoreline. Papa outran me, crashed into the waves, and joined Jesus in the demand for an encore from Holy Spirit, who immediately responded by creating a towering wave in the exact replica of Papa. The water sculpture perfectly depicted Him in a moment of pure joy, with His head tilted back, His mouth wide with laughter, and His hands high in the air. I danced and yelled in awestruck amazement at the sight of Papa formed in the waves. When the sculpture crashed down upon itself in the rhythm of the ocean, Holy Spirit swirled the funnel of water again, but this time it was a sculpture of Papa suspending Jesus in a full embrace, as if Jesus had taken a running leap into His Father's loving arms. The Triune God stood visible in a breath-taking display of unending love in this water sculpture. It only lasted a moment, and when it crashed down upon itself, Papa and Jesus were gone.

A gentle breeze blew in from the sea and I heard a whisper in the breeze saying, "The Spirit of God draws you into the deeper spiritual life…" I stood to look over the water's surface for Papa or Jesus walking toward me, but as I strained to focus on the surface of the water, a gentle wave rolled over my feet. I knew intuitively, deep in my spirit, it was the touch of Papa. I waited for another wave. Again, the touch of God wooed me. I did not know how it was possible for the Presence of God to be in the water, or for the water to become the manifest Presence of God, but I believed it was true; so I stepped into the water hip deep, where the waves break and begin the slow approach to its boundary line. I had to steady my foothold to remain on my feet. Again, the breeze rolled past me and I heard a whisper say, "Come deeper, Mat'ta. My ways are not your ways. I have more for you."

As much as I love the ocean, I also hold a healthy reverence and fear for its power; going deeper meant I must choose to trust God more than my fear. I knew it was Papa calling me deeper and that He would not harm me; going deeper was moving in faith instead of fear; my response of love to love. I walked into deeper water until the surface was even with my shoulders, past the breaking waves where the water rises and falls like lungs inhaling and exhaling.

Again, I heard the Holy Spirit say, "Come deeper, Mat'ta, I have blessing in mind, not suffering."

I stopped where I stood. Even so, my toes lifted from the ocean floor with the ebb and the flow of its breathing rhythm.

"Deeper?" Fear is only fear in the moment of its presence. I had to choose faith. It was hard, but I had to trust God over fear. The longer I stood in that place, the harder the choice would become, so I pushed off the floor of the ocean toward deeper water.

I used slow, fluid movements with my arms and legs to tread water. My logical mind began churning up reasons to fight the evidence of the supernatural. This was an ocean, after all and I cannot prolong my energy forever. Physical exhaustion was inevitable, just like death; there was no way to avoid it, was there.

Papa's voice spoke in the breeze again. "Believe. Dare to believe."

I flipped on my back, tipped my head back until my ears were under the surface of the water, and moved my arms in slow wide movements, as a butterfly does when it lights on a surface to rest. At first, my mind could only focus on the effort of survival; but within a minute or two, I relaxed. As I gazed up into the sky above me, the expanse of the heavens seemed endless. Then it occurred to me, I was as a butterfly on the surface of the ocean; only a pinpoint in the vision of an observer, impossible to see or find if one did not already know where to look. "Can you even see me, Papa?"

"I see you, Mat'ta; you are safe in my Presence." He answered.

I closed my eyes, minimized the movement of my arms, and listened to my own breathing, which seemed to be all I could hear with my ears just below the surface. Inhale. Exhale. My body and soul were at rest. Again, my logical mind threatened me that it could not last forever; but I chose faith over logic, and for now, it was enough. Inhale. Exhale. Peace washed over me. Inhale. Exhale. "Is this what it feels like to trust?" I thought.

The Spirit of God spoke again, "Mat'ta, be filled with My Spirit and His wisdom. Trust Me and come under the water."

As ridiculous as it sounded, I forgot I was floating in a vast expanse of ocean. I lifted my head and turned to look in the direction of the shore. It seemed further away than it should be. "I must be drifting." I said.

"Yes, drift. Let go of your fear. I am here. The Spirit of God surrounds you, all that I am in all of my glory; I suspend you in my tender loving care. Let go. Let Me fill you with My Spirit." Fear changed to panic as my focus moved from rest to survival, and I gave over control to my logical mind. The distance to the shore was further away than I could physically manage.

"Don't be afraid, I will not harm you. I AM the GREAT I AM. I AM the Spirit. And in this moment, I AM the water," Breath of God reassured me.

It is always like this: the voice of God, so tender and strong, speaks to me with definitive instruction and I still fight to trust. Why is that?" I ponder. "Please, help my unbelief!'

The Spirit of God said, "Trust Me. Come below the surface and breathe in, Mat'ta; find Life."

The instructions from the Holy Spirit were counter-intuitive and made no sense to me. I could not reconcile in my mind going below the water and inhaling. It was certain death. Panic settled in, I started swimming toward shore in long measured strokes and controlled breaths to conserve energy. I said to myself, "I won't make it to shore, but I will give it my best effort before I come to the end..." My thought trailed off as a revelation hit my spirit: I was preserving my own life, by my own effort, until

I came to the end of myself.

Spirit of God repeated, "Choose Me... Mat'ta, find Life."

I stopped swimming and started treading water.

"I don't understand. I thought I was born again, Papa."

"You are. This is not about your salvation. It is about dying to self. I surround you; I am with you. Let me come in and dwell within you. Your old self must die." Spirit of God's invitation was clear, but without coercion. It was my choice.

"So I can have more of you, God?" I asked.

"No, Mat'ta, so I can have more of you. I desire more of you. I must increase within you, and you must decrease. If you hold onto life just as it is, ruled by your flesh, you destroy that life; but if you surrender it, let it go, I will exchange it for my life and you will have it forever."

"More of you, less of me" I said in my mind as I inhaled deeply one last time and pushed myself under the surface of the sea. For several seconds I held that breath. Right before me, in those final seconds of my lung's ability to sustain that breath, I saw Jesus clearly formed by water, yet suspended in the water. He was transparent, but recognizable.

"Receive My Spirit." He said.

I exhaled all the air I had in my lungs. It was unto life in Christ, and unto certain death for my old nature. As I exhaled, I spoke the words, "I choose you, Jesus"; though my words were barely discernible or audible, I said them with all that I had left in me.

Jesus spoke, "Inhale, Mat'ta."

I did. I inhaled, against all logic, my lungs filled with water, just as an infant takes in amniotic fluid in the womb. I practiced breathing, one breath after another. Truly, it was a supernatural return to the womb. It made no logical sense; yet, here I was breathing freely under water. Then, right before my own eyes, I watched as my limbs and torso transform into the same transparent-type body as Jesus.

"You are filled with My Spirit, Mat'ta." Jesus said as He took my hands. The struggle was gone. The Breath of God filled me; God took up His dwelling in me. I smiled at Jesus. He smiled at me, and said, "The old is gone; the new has come. It is no longer your old nature that lives; it is the Life of Christ that lives in you."

Papa appeared. Just like Jesus, He was transparent and recognizable, but larger than I knew him to be. Papa surrounded both of us, and held us in His magnificent arms. As the overwhelmingly large mass of water formed around Papa, I knew it was the Holy Spirit. Papa held Jesus, and Jesus held me; I had no fear, even as the wave of the Spirit gathered in size and volume. We remained together; Papa, Jesus, and I suspended in the lower body of the wave, as the Holy Spirit formed the upper body of the wave into violent, rumbling rolls that cascaded and collapsed on top of each other in a display of immense power, and then gently rolled to the shoreline.

Papa still carried Jesus, and Jesus still carried me as the Spirit deposited us onto the beach. As I looked over the shoreline, it was clear to me that this was not the shore on the Garden of Mourning.

"Where are we Papa?" I asked.

He answered, "We are on the shore of the Kingdom of Your Innermost Being, Mat'ta. I am going to open your spirit's eyes and show you your truth. Then I will show you a better way."

"Papa, before we go on, can I ask you something?" I asked. He answered, "yes, of course, Mat'ta."

I knew my honest questions would not offend Papa, so I asked plainly, "I feel confused, Papa. Why did I have to inhale the water? I thought I received the Spirit when I was saved."

He answered, "let Me ask you questions, Mat'ta; one that will help you see the answer you seek. Why did you struggle in the water? Was my will unclear to you? Did you lack trust in me to keep you alive?"

"I struggled because my logical mind tells me I cannot inhale water and live."

"In other words, you had to choose between my words and the words of your own logic. Was My will unclear to you?"

I explained, "no, Your will was very clear, and I wanted to obey you. I wanted to follow your will, but I had to deny my own will to preserve my life by my own effort in order to choose your will for me to lay my life down. I had to literally choose your will instead of my will."

"Did you trust me to keep you alive?" He asked.

"I don't really know, Papa. Death was certain. Either I drowned from my efforts to save myself, or I drowned in my efforts to obey you. Either way, I had to lay down my life."

"Yes, Mat'ta, you discovered a greater truth. You cannot avoid death. Death is inevitable. Your choice is whether you will die with me, or without me. You have been mistaken in believing your choice is about living; truly living is in dying."

"That makes sense to me now that I have actually lived out the choice. My soul truly does long for you, Papa. What is best for me consumes my living. I want to do right, but I often do what I hate. It is exhausting and discouraging, Papa. There has to be more to life."

"Oh, there is so much more to life, Mat'ta, of that I assure you. I'd like to explain this spiritual truth to you through a visual reality." As He spoke, He waved His hand. What was at first a simple coastline of a beautiful beach, was now a beautiful paradise of vivid colors and sounds. A cliffside of black rock, fifty feet high or more, stood directly before us. Large boulders piled one on top of one another at the base of the cliff and jetted into the water forming a barrier to the coastline. Beautiful vines cascaded over the top of the cliff, and behind the vines were cascading streams of water.

"This cliffside is the bedrock of your spiritual life," Papa said, as He placed His hand upon the cliff wall. It stunned me how clearly I felt His touch within me as He touched the wall of the cliff.

Jesus gazed upward at the towering cliff. ""These boulders mark the time of the quaking of your faith, Mat'ta. These boulders are the broken pieces of your spiritual life." Jesus added as He climbed upon the smaller ones to reach the top of the largest boulder. "We will redeem what was lost and rebuild on this foundation. You will overcome Satan by the blood of the Lamb and the word of your testimony."

Papa walked along the cliffside until the grasslands touched the sandy shoreline. In one direction, following the coastline to the west, the grasslands eventually turned to slopes of rolling hillside.

"When we follow those slopes, we will eventually end up at the top of this cliff, Mat'ta, but for now, I have something else to reveal to you." Papa continued to walk along the cliffside until it narrowed into a valley. From my vantage point, it appeared the cliffside separated from the hillside. Deep shadows fell across the chasm between the two. Papa said, "This is the Valley of the Shadow of Death."

I peered around the corner where Papa stood at the exact opening of the valley. The shadows were deep and the darkness seemed endless, but some distance inside the mouth of the valley, I could see a very dim blue light.

"Papa, what is that blue light?" I asked as I strained to see from where it originated without entering the shadows in the valley.

"That is exactly what I want to reveal to you, Mat'ta." Papa said, but Jesus took the lead and entered the valley before us.

"Follow Me, Mat'ta, I'll show you the way. Walk where I walk," Jesus instructed as he reached over to the cliffside and pulled on a sturdy, firm vine. When it fell at His feet, He broke off a section and examined it. "Good. This makes a great rod," Jesus said, as He wacked the wood of the vine against a boulder to test its strength. When He felt satisfied with its adequacy to serve as a rod with which He could probe the shadows, He continued, "Come on Mat'ta, you have nothing to fear. I'm with you, and I'll go ahead of you."

I followed Jesus into the shadows. Papa walked behind me. It surprised me when Jesus and Papa became hard to see in the darkness.

"Why can't I see you in the darkness of these shadows?" I asked as I reached out my arms in front of me and then behind me, groping for the presence of God.

"The eyes of your spirit suffer blindness because of your disobedience and hardness of heart. A veil draped over your mind obscures the truth of the cross. The cross is everything. It is the centerpiece of our ways, Mat'ta," Jesus explained.

Papa added, "the cross holds irrevocable victory over Satan. However, Satan can distract you with the cares of this world if the cross remains displaced from the center of your spiritual life. Without the power of the cross at the core of your being, you live by religious rules. It is your law; but you have not kept the religious laws, Mat'ta. Each time you break a law, you present a legal right for an unclean spirit to harass you."

"Satan assigned tormentors to you, and then tempted you to fight against him and his minions with your flesh instead of the benefits of the cross." Jesus continued the explanation as He rustled the leaves of the blue tree to loosen the minions that hid in the tree. The minions scattered to the deeper shadows as far away from Jesus as they could manage. Jesus continued, "he took advantage of your ignorance and turned you into a doubter... an unbeliever. Unbelief weakened your faith; the supernatural power you once walked in diminished; the prayers that once produced supernatural results became fruitless. Doubt negated faith. Ultimately, his intention is to get you to destroy your own spiritual life. Unbelief and doubt accomplished his work."

As Jesus spoke, the minions He rustled loose from the blue tree cackled and sneered at me; some brazenly ventured from the deeper shadows and scurried like cockroaches along the floor of the valley. The sight of these unclean spirits and the sounds of the darkness exposed the truth of what Jesus explained. Conviction filled my soul, but I knew the safest place for me to be was as close to Jesus as I could manage, so I simply moved closer to the sound of his voice. "It is time for your return to faith. I will lead you into spiritual sight and set you free," He answered.

"Mat'ta, who do you say that I am?" Jesus asked this question to stir my profession of faith.

"You are the Son of the Living God. You are the Lamb who takes away the sin of the world. You are the Resurrection and the Life. You are the Light of the World." As I proclaimed the truth about Jesus, Jesus placed His hands over my eyes.

"Mat'ta, I fulfilled the Law. I lived perfect before My Father. My sacrifice is complete. I removed the dominion of sin over humanity. Therefore, I have the power and authority to remove the veil from your mind and remove your spiritual blindness." As He removed His hands from my eyes, I could see everything in the valley. The darkness was gone. I was appalled at the number of unclean spirits that hovered in the corners and scurried along the floor of the valley. "They are highly intelligent beings without bodies, which lurk in the darkness of your ignorance. They gain access to your kingdom through the broken-down gates of your soul. They have their own natures; all wicked, but need a human body to express their natures. They have found you to be a willing host. Unclean spirits are trespassers that take advantage of your weak will. They are the inhabitants of this present world who do the work of the devil; but do not fear, for I have overcome the world and I have come to destroy the works of the devil."

Jesus continued, "they strategize to frustrate your efforts and derail your plans for obedience to the Holy Spirit. They plot with plans to defeat you, keep you miserable and unbelieving; they make you sick, and if possible, they will kill you before your time."

"They steal what is rightfully yours. They rob you of your

peace of mind, lead you to destroy your relationships, they pummel you with guilt and shame even after Papa has forgiven your sins, and they steal the prosperity from the future we have planned for you."

"Jesus, how can so many unclean spirits find a place within me? I belong to you and the Holy Spirit dwells inside me. How can they be here?"

"Your Innermost Being is like a city, one conquered and ruled by a Tyrant named Sin. Sin took its orders from the god of this world, whose name is the Prince of the Power of the Air, the spirit that works in the children of wrath. These gangs of tormentors are the Tyrant's army. They have occupied your city for most of your life. They remain in place because of the culture of sin within your soul. That culture is maintained by feeding from the tree of the prince's nature, which strengthens your rebellion, disobedience, and carnality."

Suddenly, as Jesus spoke, a large blue tree with three separate types of fruit, illuminated with intense light. Within the fruit of the tree, I could see the seeds of various shades of blue light. "This Tree produces the seeds of Sin's nature."

A whining sound, like a dissident chord, emanated from this

tree. It sounded neither like the songs of heaven I heard in the Garden of Mourning, or the songs Odunay sang over me in the center of the Tempest.

"Why have I not heard this song before, Jesus?"

He answered, "today you have grown hungry for another type of fruit, the Fruit of the Holy Spirit. Spiritual fruit brings death to this tree and its works. The song you hear comes from your soul, which remains unsubmitted to the Holy Spirit, and whines like a rebellious child. If you pamper your sin-trained soul and give in to its demands, its rebellion against God strengthens. Your soul recognizes this tree and its fruit, Mat'ta. Unless the Holy Spirit restores your soul, your soul will continually lead you back to this tree. You need to understand, Mat'ta, this tree is not your old nature. Papa executed your old nature on Calvary. Crucifixion removed sin's dominion over you. I became the rightful ruler of Your Innermost Being, and my throne is located in your spirit. Think of your spirit as the center of this Kingdom where the Worship Center, Divine Courtroom, and Holy Palace of the King are located. Your spirit was full of darkness before I moved in; now, it is full of light, as the city that sits on a hill; on the top of this cliff," Papa said as He walked over to the cliff's wall and placed his hand on it. "The unclean spirits avoid the top of this cliff, but they still roam the territories of your soul and the outlands of your body. As you choose to surrender more of your inner kingdom to me, I evict the gangs of intruders out of your kingdom, deport them back to where I commanded them to be from the beginning, and rebuild your infrastructure, body, soul, and spirit. It is a judicial process." Papa walked back to where I stood and said, "I will train you to participate in the judicial process until your kingdom is under the dominion of My Spirit. Then you will be truly free. We will begin with this ancient tree whose seed came from the Serpent."

I examined the tree. Each fruit was distinctly and mysteriously attractive. My spirit recoiled from its aroma and told me to walk away and never return. My soul growled with hunger pangs.

As I focused on the first fruit, I heard the Holy Spirit whisper to me, "eating of this Tree puts you at war with me."

The first fruit smelled similar to fresh citrus; clean, crisp and sweet all at the same time, but it was not of a citrus I recognized. Its aroma had an alluring effect on my soul; almost like a promise that if I partook of it, I would possess the power of influence: who I was, what I did, and what I said would be impactful in the lives of other people. People would follow me and celebrate me; I could be somebody.

"This fruit is called Pride of Life. It empowers self-promotion. It feeds your hunger for glory. It tempts you to exalt yourself over others, to deem yourself more important than others. When people threaten your position of importance, this fruit strengthens your cunning motives, and retrieves the training you have in stirring up discord, strife, jealousy, wrath, and divisions. These works of the flesh become attitudes of hatred and unforgiveness; the culture of your soul, mind, and emotions become the fortresses for the tormentors." The unclean spirits constrained in the corner of the shadows above the tree cackled and sneered at me as Holy Spirit spoke. "These tormentors take advantage of your wounds of rejection. They do all they can to block your will to repent of pride. They use lies and painful emotions to convince you of your right to offense. They know they retain their legal right to torment you as long as unforgiveness remains in you. While they are at it, they lead you into destructive habits."

"No wonder I constantly fall into struggles. I crave this fruit, especially when someone threatens to reject me or exclude me," I said to myself.

"My Fruit of the Spirit trains you in love, peace, long-suffering, and meekness. Papa wants you to be in healthy relationship with others," Holy Spirit said, "I empower you to love God with all your heart, soul, and mind; and to love your neighbor as yourself. I will visit each wound of rejection, and strengthen your resolve to forgive, just as Papa has forgiven you, then we can restore your soul and renew a right spirit within you."

My taste for this blue fruit waned. Now that I knew the fruit of this tree was manifest temptation, I approached the second fruit with more caution. It smelled similar to tropical fruits: coconut, mango, and banana. Its fragrance carried me directly into the temptation for 'more' of every excess pleasure and a promise that I would never suffer want again.

Papa said, "This fruit is called Lust of the Flesh. It empowers all forbidden desires. Sins of lust bring decay and eventually destruction to your body."

The Tormentors named Perversion, Guilt, and Addictions laughed in mockery as Holy Spirit described their stronghold, "Guilt leads this gang of Tormentors through cunning tricks that encourage you to judge yourself 'permanently polluted' long after I have cleansed you. He whips you with debilitating shame."

Now it made sense why it seemed impossible for me to rid myself of guilt. I eat this fruit to numb my shame, not realizing it fuels guilt instead. I confessed, "it is true: in my head I know I am forgiven; in my emotions I still suffer shame. It is hard for me to believe or accept myself as the holy vessel you require of me."

"Do you not know you are the temple of God? I created you for me, not for lust. You are my home, Mat'ta; you cannot make yourself holy through good behavior. Only I make you holy and blameless, a pure, set-apart-child of God. Your slavery to Guilt can end. As I restore your soul through the atonement of my blood, you will be holy as I am holy. My fruit of kindness, goodness, and self-control will empower you to overcome the lust of the flesh. You will lose your taste for sin."

My appetite for this fruit waned as well. It was familiar and a part of my regular diet; but with Papa's words, I felt more empowered to resist it and choose better.

"Mat'ta, lust manifests in many ways. What do you covet? What do you demand?" He asked questions that were not really questions at all. As Holy Spirit spoke, a third fruit began to glow more brightly. I turned back to the tree, against my better judgment, and reached for the glowing fruit buried deeper in the foliage of the tree. It differed slightly in color and tone, more of a deep violet-red. It was out of my reach and I could not touch it, but my head fit perfectly between the other fruit, so I leaned in to inhale its fragrance of wild berries, something like raspberry, blueberry, and acai. "My favorites," I said aloud. I inhaled again; this time the fragrance penetrated deep into my soul. I recognized this fruit, I knew its scent, and recalled its flavor.

"This fruit is called Lust of the Eye." Tormentors named Envy, Jealousy, Gluttony, and Selfishness cackled and sneered, sensing their imminent exposure. "Whatever you covet, or strongly desire, that belongs to someone else and you look upon with your eyes with lust, this becomes a trap for your soul. These traps of covetousness are tethered to the taproot of this tree, which leaches the spiritual life out of the soil of your soul."

"Tethered to a taproot?" I pondered, as I felt the cravings within me increasing.

"Yes and it has a name," Papa said.

"What is that, Papa?" I said as I wrestled with the temptation to gorge myself on this fruit.

Holy Spirit answered loudly, within me, and around me, "Independence from God." His words vibrated the foundations of my humanity. I backed my head out of the tree so quickly and so abruptly, my movement knocked the fruit loose from its branch, along with the other fruits that had tempted me. Losing my balance, I fell backward to the ground just as the freed fruit landed in my lap. There in my lap was all the fruit on which I feast. I sat up on my knees and bent forward to inhale the meal in front of me. The seeds of each fruit were the same deep blue light, regardless of their various shade differences, or the nature of lust. I do not know why I had not noticed before this moment, but the seed within me, at the center of my torso just above my stomach was also this same deep blue. I looked up from the fruit to find Jesus kneeling beside me.

"Is this the Tree of the Knowledge of Good and Evil, Lord?" I asked.

Jesus answered in a soft voice, "no, Mat'ta, it is The Serpent's Tree of Fleshly Desires."

"Why does this tree live?" I asked.

Jesus answered me, "you falsely believe you receive nourishment from this tree. Reality is quite the opposite. It receives its nourishment from you. Every time you eat its fruit, you sow its seed in the fertile soil of your unsubmitted soul. It can only survive in the soil where sin feeds its roots, and produces corruption."

I interrupted, "if I quit eating its fruit, the tree will die."

"No, living life by the law… do this, do not do that… will only show you where you fail to live in perfection, the lust and temptation will increase. If you turn your focus on the health of your spirit, you will live by the Spirit. You will be free!"

Jesus added, "I do not have religious rules in mind for you. Hunger and thirst, but hunger after Me, Mat'ta, and I will satisfy you completely. Nourished by the fruit of the Spirit, you will start acting as I do. Your yoke of slavery to sin will snap and fall away. You will change! Where the Spirit of the Lord is, there is liberty."

Holy Spirit added, "if you want freedom in your life, we need to be in union; we need to talk continually. I will lead you into all truth, and reveal to you the things to come. We, the Godhead, are eternal. We are in your past, we are in your present, and we are in your future simultaneously, Mat'ta. We know where you have been and exactly how to get to where you want you to be. Our plans for you are full of goodness because we delight in you. We know what needs developed within you, the skills, the experiences, and the spiritual wisdom you need to operate and flourish in your future. We want our conversations to be preoccupied with these plans. We have so much to do. Do you understand?"

"Yes… finally, I do understand. Why do I have the blue seed only right here?" I asked.

"Because you are redeemed, Mat'ta, but your unsubmitted soul rules your life and lords over your spirit. As you feed on the fruit of your fleshly desires, corruption and deceit increase, and you long for independence from God." The Lord of Heaven, by the Spirit of Truth, summed up my condition. My iniquity was before me, in the form of a tree full of fruit I feast on day after day. In the exposing light of truth, I desperately begged for intervention. "Cut it down! Please, uproot it! Do something!"

Jesus answered, "I already have, Mat'ta. I carried this Tree to the Hill of Golgotha."

Papa said, "its nature had nothing in My Beloved Son. I choked the life out of the seed of the Serpent, as My Son willingly became the sin offering. He conquered death and the Adamic spirit by remaining in perfect union with us in every thought, every action, every word, and every motive, from his first breath to his last. He conquered the Adamic soul by choosing my will over His own. He conquered the Adamic body by taking the wrath for sin into His own body, and poured out His blood as an offering."

The Holy Spirit declared boldly, "The Life of a sacrifice is in the blood; The Blood of Jesus is perfect. It did not cover sin, as did the blood of rams and goats in the old covenant; it removed sin, once and forever!" As He said 'once and forever', a deep quake shook the foundations under our feet. Whatever not built on the foundation of rock fell under the force of God's words. I felt and heard the destruction of fortresses and strongholds, but from where I stood, I only witnessed the splitting of the soil at the base of the blue tree. I dropped to my hands and knees, then all the way to my stomach as I watched the tree topple from its foundation; three roots, fully exposed along with the taproot, which showed clear signs of terminal decay.

I laid face down on the ground, trembling with the Fear of the Lord even after the shaking ceased. Until this moment, the Living God had dealt with me in gentleness; but now I lay prostrated in the Presence of the Living God as the Fear of the Lord advanced as a tsunami wave. The Fear of the Lord and its cleansing power crashed onto the shores of the island of My Innermost Being, and flooded the inland territory. The forceful wave swept me up and churned me in its rolling billows along with the debris of the Kingdom, but I remained unharmed. The wisdom of God was clear to me: I could breathe under the surface of the waves in this moment because I had surrendered to the will of God in the water earlier. Full of vigor and renewed strength, I tumbled in graceful loops within the violent wave, unafraid, full of confidence that this tsunami was the goodness of God. With that revelation, reverence, and awe for God surged through my body, and exploded into worship as I pumped my arms and legs with all the strength I had in the direction of the water's surface. I felt the surging power of the Holy Spirit beneath me, and in one movement, I shot out of the water high in the air, like a bird taken to flight suspended on the wind. "God is great!" I declared, as the Holy Spirit declared, "those who hope in the Lord will renew their strength. They will soar on wings like eagles; they will run and not grow weary; they will walk and not be faint."

Together, Holy Spirit and I soared over the island. I examined the aftermath of the cleansing tsunami as the waters receded. I recognized the original construction of some strongholds even through the remaining rubble. In many cases, I was elated to see the destruction. I had built these fortresses for the sole purpose of insulating my heart from rejection and exclusion; I barricaded myself from both sources of suffering, but created a life of isolation. Through the rubble, I could see the parts of my person I once valued, the parts that uniquely represented my authentic contribution in relationship.

"Mat'ta, I see remnants of the best you. Would you like me to free them from the wreckage?"

"Yes, Holy Spirit! Yes, please set me free."

Holy Spirit blew, and a gentle breeze carried away the sand and dust of the wreckage. I could feel imagination, creativity, and courageous strength rising up within me. I felt my innate playfulness and joy restored. Clearly, these attributes were the foundations of my child-like faith and my spiritual gifts.

I said, "this time, Holy Spirit, I put these parts of me into your hands. Please, take them as my offering."

At the conclusion of my words, Holy Spirit dropped a pillar of flame over the remnants. When the holy fire consumed my offering, in its place stood a very large crystal arrow that pointed to the cliff of my spiritual life.

Holy Spirit sealed the moment by saying, "Now, the best of you will be a marker along the road of salvation. When others see your life, and hear your testimony, they'll find a path that leads to Jesus."

Chapter Eight

THE SHORELINE

Holy Spirit said, "you are ready for the shoreline, Mat'ta."

The force of the wind on which I floated changed, and I descended until my feet hit the shore in a run. I could see Papa and Jesus waiting for us in the distance. As I slowed to a walk, I came to the rubble of a building. The sign, which once hung over the doorway of the building, was clearly visible. Jesus stepped up onto the rubble. I followed Him so that I could get a better view of the writing. Shockingly, it was the name of my home church. Sadness and grief rose up in my heart, tears filled my eyes, but deep in my spirit, I knew why this building lay in ruins. As I stood contemplating those reasons, the rubble began shifting and disintegrating into sand and dust. Jesus and I stood together in its remains. He took my hand to comfort me, but I turned to Him, buried my face in His chest, and cried. I truly loved this church, and grieved its death almost as long as I grieved the death of my miscarried children. I felt Jesus inhale deeply. Over my shoulder, as He held me tightly to His chest, He exhaled and the dust of the remains blew away.

He whispered in my ear, "anything built from ambition, any work that glorifies humans, will not last."

He released His embrace and turned me around; before me stood a large metal tree. Its roots, anchored to the exposed bedrock of the shoreline, supported the massive trunk. Carved into the trunk of the tree were names of the church's founding families along with their children, grandchildren, and great-grandchildren's names. The names of families and the individuals the founders led to salvation formed the boughs of the tree. Their children and descendants of the extended family members formed the large branches, which continued to expand until all showed the way in which each individual found their way into the family.

Holy Spirit read each name aloud. He swirled and breathed on each name as he commented with words full of love and recognition of each person. When he reached the upper branches, he said, "look Mat'ta, here is your name." He breathed on the etching and my name glowed within the heated metal. There, too, were the names of my husband and each of our children. I must have had a look of surprise on my face when He read the names of my children.

Jesus said, "Mat'ta, your church family embraced each one of your children. They joined you in your hope for their survival; they grieved with you in their deaths. They shared in your suffering, just as you shared in their sufferings."

"I miss our home," I said, "after all this time, so many of us have not found another tribe where we feel knit together with the people, as we did here."

"I miss our home too, Mat'ta. To this day, old friends still reminisce about the beauty of that divine fellowship. On the occasion when they are together, true bonds of life remain between us all, and we feel like we have come home." Holy Spirit added, "our tribe discovered true Koinonia. It is only a taste of what heaven is like."

Before this moment, it had never crossed my mind that Holy Spirit was homesick for our gatherings as much as I was.

"I know you are with all Believers, Holy Spirit, but it really matters that you loved our tribe; that we were a place you longed to be as much as we did," I said with real, sincere gratitude in my heart. Holy Spirit continued His intentional examination of the family tree as I spoke. He began reading other names to me. Some names strummed my heartstrings, and caused my spirit to well up with gratitude for their influence in my life. Some names stirred reverence and respect because they belonged to the spiritual giants that trained me up in the Word of God, accepted me into their homes, taught me the ways of the Kingdom, and convinced me that I belonged.

"I love them all so much, Holy Spirit. Some have been gone for many years now, but they live boldly in my memories. I still draw courage from them."

Holy Spirit moved to the next bough and its branches. Every name was someone Noel and I loved sacrificially; some we led to faith in Jesus, and they grew into leaders of the tribe. They were dear friends, but turned against us when the destruction began. The pain felt like a millstone of offense around my neck. Because of the shame I still carried, I expected Holy Spirit to pick it up and throw it into the sea, dragging me with it. In these painful years of my life, I threw off restraint and over-responded in fleshly attacks. Lost in the heaviness of the emotion that accompanied these memories, I missed when the Holy Spirit moved over to the branch on the opposite side of the family tree. He began to read the names. A whirlwind of emotion swirled up inside me, just as it always did when I thought on these people.

"Slow down, Mat'ta" He said as He moved away from the tree and hovered over me directly. Papa added, "I'm here with you. It will not overcome you, not this time. Take a deep breath. Trust Me."

Holy Spirit moved back to the tree, back to the same names, and began examining them. He pointed out that each name had a black spot, a rotten place that threatened to sever it from its branch of the tree. Every name on the branch and the shoots coming from the branch suffered from these rotten spots. The spots were not present because of their lacking; their lacking is not my business, nor is it my place to judge their condition. The spots were the infection caused by my hatred and unforgiveness. I had harmed them.

"Mat'ta, tell me about this side of the tree." I sensed deep grief from the Holy Spirit; it was not my grief, but His grief I sensed, and that changed everything I was going to say.

"I will, Holy Spirit, but you speak first. I sense your grief. Your heart is broken over this part of our history." I said.

"Mat'ta, you see these people through your lenses. They see

you through their lenses. None of you sees through my lenses," He said with brokenness in His tone.

At the most destructive point in the history of our tribe, when factions were splintering our union, and death of our divine fellowship was imminent, Papa joined me on a walk. The memory came back as if I was reliving it. I was walking alone on the road that leads to my home, worshipping, struggling to focus on Papa instead of the contemptuous attacks exchanged that day. I was desperate to break free from the hatred I felt imprisoning my soul. As I prayed, I asked Papa to take away my pain and hatred. He instructed me to bless my enemies but I emphatically refused to do so.

Just that day, hours earlier, the tribe's leader removed me from the fellowship of the tribe. He had been the one misled by the Advisor, a man he believed was going to take our family into new places, but he saw me as the roadblock on the path to his new-and-improved kingdom. I met with him to warn him of the fruit of division surrounding this Advisor, but before I could finish my words, the blame, squarely placed on my shoulders with one sentence, landed with a weight I could not bear. "You are the problem." He, as my spiritual authority, spoke my prison sentence with his judicial authority. I attempted a rebuttal; he silenced me as he placed additional restrictions over me.

"Holy Spirit, not only was this sentence unjust, it was coming from someone I had served alongside my entire spiritual life. He was my friend. He was my shepherd. Worst yet, I knew ambition blinded him. He did not see what was going on around him; but he is not all to blame; he could not hear my words because my carnal behavior spoke too loudly. I had added to the division."

"I know, Mat'ta. I intended to administer justice that day," He said.

I admitted, "you would have done so if I had blessed my enemies as you instructed."

"I gave the same opportunity that very day to every name on this tree branch," He said as He traced His fingers over each name. "No one picked up the cause. Instead, some celebrated your demise and claimed it as their personal victory. Some saw the injustice of the sentence against you, but lacked the courage to stand up in righteousness for fear of similar consequences. Some, like you, let your hearts petrify into stone with deep-seated hatred."

"I'm deeply sorry I grieved you. I'm sorry we all grieved you," I said with sincere regret.

Holy Spirit continued, "it was the work of Satan when your leader declared his judicial sentence, and he placed that weight of responsibility for the destruction of his kingdom upon you. Satan intended to completely destroy you."

"Even under the pain of rejection, I knew it was the work of Satan. I tried to separate my pain from my intercession, because I knew our tribe was dying; but I was not spiritually mature enough to know how to engage in the necessary warfare against Satan without attacking flesh and blood. I really messed things up, more than once, which is why I still struggle with such a sense of responsibility for our tribe's death," I confessed.

Jesus moved next to me and said, "you were like a Maverick, kicking and fighting against everyone that came near your paddock. You were so enflamed with betrayal, you harmed yourself in your efforts to throw off restraint, and remove the bit I placed in your mouth to control your tongue. I restrained you because I love you, and I wanted to minimize how the darkness worked through you."

I agreed and said, "I remember fighting you, Lord. I was overcome with a sense of injustice."

Jesus continued, "I attempted to enter the paddock, to penetrate your place of isolation so that I could speak softly to you, to tend your wounds; wounds you caused yourself, and wounds inflicted upon you. I brought healing salve, and a few trustworthy tribe members to sit with you."

I rebutted, "I know you did. I treasured those friends, but I still lost most of those relationships in the process." I admitted with deep sadness and regret.

"Even with time, you were not healing, not even with the loving care of your best friend. So, I removed you completely from the territory, with a promise that when this sifting by Satan ended, you would call on me, and return to strengthen your brother." Everything Jesus said to me was true. It felt good to have it in the open and no longer swirling around in the darkness of my soul.

"Has the sifting ended?" I asked.

"Have you forgiven and blessed your enemies?" He rebutted.

"Yes, you know how I have labored over this, Lord." I responded then turned to Papa.

"Papa, you refused imperfect forgiveness from me. You taught me how to bless others by creating lack in my life."

Papa added, "yes, as you prayed and asked why so much of your life eroded, I showed you it was the result of unforgiveness. I reminded you that if you do not forgive the debt of others, you remain unforgiven of your debt. We took no pleasure in your condition, but when you repeatedly refused our prodding to forgive your enemies, we knew the tormentors would have to complete their work."

I stumbled along the path of unforgiveness for a long time. It was a hard, difficult path to walk, and it led me into the Serpent's Valley the day I realized my life with Papa would never repair until I forgave my enemies. This was the requirement of righteousness I fought against the hardest. My refusal to forgive was set in pride; my pride drew destruction to my life. Papa turned me over to the torment of the yipping Hunters, who led me into the Oasis, where I nearly lost all spiritual life until I drank from the Fount of Blessing. It was at the Fount of Blessing I cried out in repentance of my pride and all I had done. The Fountain refreshed my soul until I surged with renewed strength to run home to Papa. I set my sight on the Great Wall as I ran from the Oasis, but I struggled to find the Eastern Pass. The Hunters were in constant pursuit of me; I often found myself running in circles. On occasion, I would return to the edge of the Oasis in search of landmarks that looked familiar in hopes of finding the original trail I followed the day I entered the Valley. I would hunt for the bubbling spring so that I could drink from it before running on. I discovered it only sprung up when I verbally proclaimed blessings. At first, I blessed Noel and those friends that remained faithful to us. The Fount of Blessing surged with renewed power, enough to provide water to drink and to bathe. Over time, I discovered blessing my enemies released the Fountain into its full glorious expression. The more time I spent in the Fountain declaring sincere blessing over my enemies, the deeper the cleansing waters reached into my soul. Eventually, I was free from unforgiveness.

I concluded, "now, I bless my enemies as brothers; I bless them the way I would want to be blessed, and if there is something I am missing, I want to know so that I can rectify that lacking too."

"Then it is time to put this to rest, Mat'ta." He touched the Family Tree. Every name turned red hot, even the names that had dark spots within them. Before the Tree cooled and hardened into purified gold, He said, "The gates of hell have come against My Church, but even with all its force of power, it has not prevailed. The works done in ambition and the kingdoms of men, including your own works, have blown away. What remains is eternal. What remains is my Body."

He waited as I examined the Tree. The black spots remained. As I reached to touch the spot in the name of the Advisor, the one person I held as responsible for the destruction of our tribe, He asked me, "do you love Me, Mat'ta?"

"You know that I love you, Lord." I replied.

"Then bless your enemies until you see restoration to every name on this tree."

Jesus stood facing me, and took my hands into His hands. He placed my hands over the scars he bore on His own face. Leaving my hands in place, He placed His hands over the scars on my face.

"These scars mark where you goaded against my restraints, and fought my loving touch to break your resistance for your own safety; but you see, I bear the same scars, Mat'ta. I took them to the cross with me. I bore the curse spoken over you; it hung on the Tree at Calvary. In this moment, eternity touches you as I absorb the judgment of that curse and remove the judicial authority it carried." As Jesus spoke the words, the scars on His face and the scars on my face lit up with glory for just a moment. "Mat'ta, it is finished." I knew I was free.

"The Serpent intended to stop Spirit-led prayer, to stop its authoritative results. He was not successful. The Sifting is over. Be strengthened and pray for My Body. Start with the names on this Family Tree. When you have learned my ways in prayer, turn and strengthen others." Jesus put His hand on the trunk of the metal Tree. When He pushed against the Family Tree, it fell over and became a Bridge that led from the seashore to the top edge of the cliff of my spiritual life.

"Soon we will cross this bridge, Mat'ta, so that we can reveal our greatest gift to you; but before we leave the shoreline, I want to examine this final structure," Jesus said as He moved to the edge of a crystal, clear baby crib.

I approached the crib for a closer examination. To my surprise, it was a crib with a replica of the Teddy Bear given to me as a gift after the miscarriage of my twins. Remembering the moment stirred familiar emotions and it became clear to me that this event was a pivotal, defining moment in my life.

"Mat'ta, I am with you. Do not avoid the truth. There is nothing here that overcomes me; but it is time to face what overcomes you."

I invited Holy Spirit, Papa, and Jesus to the edge of the crib. As God examined the detail of the structure, I experienced Him as the God of Peace who offered healing and restoration.

"I remember this moment, Mat'ta, as the moment when your heart split open. In the invisible realm, this moment was a crossroad," Papa said, as He admired the detail and artistry of the crib. I felt no judgment, even though infertility had been my excuse for my own judgment against God. He examined the crib as the representation of my suffering in order to remove what does not belong. His goodness was searching for what was missing or what needed restoring. "It seems to Me, Mat'ta, our time together with your children has brought a deep healing to your wounds. This structure is made of diamond formed under the pressure of suffering. It survived the wave of the Fear of the Lord because it stands on the foundation of rock. You have labored in prayer over your infertility. We have cleansed you. It is a memorial that marks your experience, but it no longer holds grief."

It was true. As He so intimately moved over the crib and Teddy Bear, I experienced hope and true comfort, a comfort starkly different from the numbing escapism I once experienced.

"I am healed and changed," I said with delighted surprise in that instant.

"Mat'ta, tell me about the Teddy Bear." He already knew the significance of the Teddy Bear, but my telling of the story would help me accept His healing and restorative work.

"You remember, Lord. You gave it to me two days after the miscarriage of the twins." This pregnancy was the one Noel and I risked involving others through their prayer and support. I carried these babies longer than any other pregnancy; we allowed hope to enter our hearts, believing our arms would be full with children we desperately longed for.

On the day the babies died, we were devastated. Noel, grieving in desperate pain himself, literally carried me when my grief was so heavy it felt impossible to walk. He said to me in that moment, "Mat'ta, our future must require the strength of character that can only be forged by this kind of pain."

I knew he was right, and I submitted to his wisdom; but deep grief overwhelmed me. I felt myself falling into the dark night of my soul. Two nights later, after Noel had fallen asleep, I sat awake, moaning in physical and emotional pain, crying out to Papa with one repeated question, "what do I do with these empty arms? They were supposed to be full."

Moments later, there was a knock on my door. At first, I thought I was hearing things. It was nearly midnight, and not logical that someone was knocking; I waited to see if it would happen again. When I heard the knocking a second time, I opened the door to find a beautiful Latino woman standing in front of me with a Teddy Bear extended toward me. I did not know her, she did not know me, we did not speak the same language; but in one gesture, she communicated everything that needed saying. She insisted I take the Teddy Bear from her, and then she pointed up.

I said, "from God?" as I pointed up to clarify what I believed she was saying.

She nodded her head yes, said, "Papa" then she simply walked away. I thanked her with tears in my eyes, closed the door, and slid my back down the door until I rested on the floor. I held that Teddy Bear to my chest as I realized that the God of the Universe had orchestrated the timing of this beautiful gift with the timing of my heart's outcry.

"God gave me a Teddy Bear," I said aloud as the impossible met my grief. In my arms was a beautiful white Teddy Bear, holding a red heart that read 'I love you'. God filled my empty arms in that desperate moment with a physical gift I could hold. He was inviting me to find all comfort in Him. For a time, I did, but as it would prove out, the desperately painful circumstances of our life following this miscarriage drowned out the voice of the Comforter.

"I know there is more to this season of your life, but these other circumstances are not connected to your children, Mat'ta. Because you have bound the loss of your children to other circumstances of injustice, you have believed the Serpent's lie that I am an Unjust, Cruel Master." Holy Spirit's words were bold, but as I accepted them, they represented exactly what I came to think and feel. "Let's separate the loss of your children from the other circumstances so that I can put my seal on your healing and make good out of your loss. My seal marks this territory of your innermost being as 'Conquered by God' and warns the unclean spirits that the Kingdom of Heaven is near." "Yes! Yes, please!" I could feel victory and freedom rising up in my mind.

Together, the Godhead encased the entire structure within in a funnel of lights made with the colors of a rainbow. I was awestruck by God's expression of His own majestic beauty in the light and the promise of fertility that hovered over the crib.

"Mat'ta, you and Noel will conceive twin boys. You will raise them in the knowledge of God. They will be strong-willed, natural leaders. You will have to drive folly and rebellion out of their hearts; along the way, they will test you, and at times, they will pierce your heart. Your love for them will sustain you through times of great struggles. When they are grown, they will turn their hearts back toward you and Noel, and take up the prophetic calling I now declare over them. They will be born into a time of history when lawless, wicked, evildoers will dominate the culture of the world. They will struggle with the many temptations that define this culture. They will strive to minimize the chasm that lays between the men which you raised them to be and those with whom they seek their belonging. Take heart, I will be with them. They are mine, before they are yours. Noel will consecrate them as part of the Elijah and Elisha generation. He has laid down his own life and all his dreams to answer the call I have placed on him in order to lead these two powerful men of God. Noel and your sons will heed the call to stand apart from the culture of the world. Together, they will face the enemies of God as victorious warriors. They will witness great miracles. I will baptize them in the Holy Spirit, and empower them to live courageously. The end of their lives will far exceed the miraculous power it will take to bring them through physical birth. Your womb is hostile and unfit for pregnancy; in spite of this condition, you will give birth and bear witness to the supernatural power of God. Their birth will always be the beginning testimony that overcomes the Serpent; and your children will be the crown you lay at my feet."

I responded humbly, "thank you, Papa, for this promise" as my heart surged with joy and anticipation of motherhood.

"Mat'ta, every experience of your life has the potential to become the crystal stepping stones on the road that leads others to the Kingdom of God. You bear the scars of suffering for the good of others. Your suffering is priceless. When you allow me to purify it, I can illuminate it with my glory and use your story to guide others into salvation. Your story becomes my story." The Holy Spirit's revelation was so magnificent within my heart, I willingly submitted my will and emotion to Him. His ways, His will, His purposes were my desire. "Whatever you want, I surrender to you." As I made this profession, I heard a violent crack followed by a thundering crash from the direction of the Valley of the Shadow of Death. We all looked in the direction of the sound; however, while I was still attempting to identify its source, Papa and Jesus were dancing and rejoicing with such abandon I felt embarrassed that I did not understand why. Holy Spirit swirled around me and under me, lifting me into flight. Within moments, we approached the mouth of the Valley just in time to witness the unclean spirits scurry onto the shoreline. Papa and Jesus stood together, defending the shoreline.

Independence from God, the unclean spirit of highest ranking, said in a loud growl, "what do we have to do with you, Son of God. Would you expel us before our time?"

"Be muzzled to silence and come out of her." Jesus commanded. In that instance, every unclean spirit disappeared. I did not know where they went, or how they got out, but they were most definitely gone.

Holy Spirit continued the flight into the Valley until He set me down gently at the base of the blue tree. It had fallen over with such force, all four roots severed. Clearly displayed in each root were carved words: 'I will', 'I want', 'I think', and on the taproot it said 'I exalt'.

"I am crucified with Christ; it is no longer I that live, but Christ who lives in me…" Holy Spirit declared the words written by the apostle Paul. Jesus and Papa walked around the corner of the Valley, dressed in military uniforms. As they approached the fallen tree, they both drew their swords high over their heads and began severing limbs and branches.

As they worked, they both quoted Hebrews 4:12, "For the word of God is alive and active; sharper than any two-edged sword, it penetrates even to dividing soul from spirit, joint from marrow; it judges the thoughts and intentions of the heart." With only a few precise swings, they had reduced the tree to the shape of a cross. All that remained was the root system.

Papa stepped up on the horizontal arms of the cross and said, "it is my will that you seek first the Kingdom of God and His righteousness, and all things will be added unto you." It was clear He was taking the land of my kingdom for Himself in response to my surrender of my will. "Mat'ta, I stand at the horizontal bar of this cross where my will meets your will."

Jesus stepped next to me and said, "deny yourself, take up your cross and follow me." He handed me His sword and I knew exactly what I had to do. I stepped up on the vertical trunk of the cross and proclaimed as I took violent swings at the root of the tree with the engraving 'I exalt' in its flesh, "Carnal flesh, and the nature of rebellion, is enmity against God. It cannot please God; the only solution is death!" As the sword severed the taproot, the tree released a discernible exhale, proof that it was not a tree at all but part of my person.

Next, I proclaimed, "may I never boast of knowledge except in the cross of my Lord Jesus Christ, through which the world has been crucified to me, and I to the world!" as I swung the sword at the root engraved, 'I think'. I willfully rejected the humanistic philosophies, the worldly education, and the entertainment that stood contrary to the Word of God. "If I am blind to something else I have not mentioned here, Holy Spirit, please reveal it to me so I can reject it too."

Next, I proclaimed, "he who does the will of God abides forever. I choose your will Papa, over my will!" as I swung the sword at the root engraved with 'I will'.

Finally, I proclaimed one last proclamation, "I will do nothing out of selfish ambition and vain conceit; rather, I will value others above myself, not looking for my interests, but the interests of others. I choose your mindset, Jesus!" as I swung the sword at the root engraved 'I want'. With the final blow of the sword, the cross broke free from the root system.

Jesus moved toward me. I handed the sword back to Him before He assisted me down from the trunk of the tree. "We are so pleased with you, Mat'ta. Pick up your cross and follow me."

Chapter Nine

THE CROSS

Jesus placed the weight of one side of the cross on his shoulder and back, I put the weight of the other side of the cross on my shoulder and back. Together, we carried the burdensome cross to the base of the metal tree. It was clear Jesus intended to climb the tree, with the cross, up the tree to the top of the cliff of my Spiritual Life. He could see me struggling to bear the weight of the tree, so He and Papa bore the bulk of the burden.

"The work of the cross has already been done for you; this is the work of the cross in you." Jesus said as we crested the top edge of the metal tree.

At the top of the cliff, at the highest point of the land, Holy Spirit swirled as a funnel of fire. Papa and Jesus lifted the cross and carried it the remainder of the distance, into the holy fire.

The Godhead, as one expression, but in three distinct voices proclaimed, "The God of Peace sanctifies you through and through. Your whole spirit, soul, and body made blameless at the coming of the Lord Jesus Christ. The One who calls you is faithful, and He will do it."

The foundations of my being, in me and around me, shook violently with every word spoken by God. I bowed low and lay on my belly prostrated in reverence as The Fear of the Lord moved over the surface of the land. Towering rock formations and cliffs rose and formed the walls of a fortress where the shoreline once existed. The Valley of the Shadows of Death closed tight with the shifting movement as new mountains formed.

The funnel of fire expanded until it consumed the entire surface on the top of the Cliff of my Spiritual Life. I remained prostrated as the fire passed over me. I felt no pain, but my entire being shook and trembled in the Presence of the Living God. The names of God flowed out of my mouth, one after another, and became seed sown in the soil of my innermost being. Places that had previously been bare or scarce were now fertile; new trees and flowers sprung up from the ground and filled these places.

The word from Isaiah 11 welled up in my heart and burst out of my mouth as a bolt of lightning with each word, "The Spirit of the Lord rests on Jesus; the Spirit of wisdom and understanding, the Spirit of counsel and might, the Spirit of knowledge and the fear of the Lord." As I concluded the scripture, a massive tree, fully matured and filled with fruit, rose from the ground with a loud rumbling sound.

The tree was fully erected and firmly set in its place as Papa commanded, "let there be light!" The Tree, called Spiritual Life, illuminated with God's glory; the entire tree became translucent. The Breath of God blew over the tree, as the Holy Spirit whispered, "God Seed"; every atom in The Great Tree became a seed suspended in the breath of God, obedient to the voice of the Creator.

I repeated Holy Spirit's words, "God-Seed" as I pondered what I was witnessing. The atoms in all living things existed because He spoke them into existence; and they responded to His voice because He is the Author of Life.

As I moved to a kneeling position and raised my hands in worship, I could see the atoms, the God-Seed, which formed my own body illuminated with His glory. Simple revelation hit my conscious mind: Created in the image of God, animated by the breath of God, filled with His Spirit, I am the temple of God, His dwelling.

The branches of The Great Tree were full of magnificent, beautiful clusters of small orbs of light that looked like glass, but similar in texture to grapes. Each orb of one cluster varied in color, and each cluster varied in color from the next; it reminded me of the tapestry of Papa's Robe of Righteousness, yet far more varied in shades. Within the trunk of the tree were winding stands; something like the strands of human DNA, but it was not human.

I asked myself, "what are these winding strands?" The question was a thought, not spoken.

Holy Spirit whispered in response, "Spiritual Life."

"Spiritual Life" I repeated.

"Yes, Mat'ta, only Spiritual Life produces spiritual fruit, it is your nourishment. I AM spiritual life. I AM the fruit. When you experience Me, you taste My affection and charity toward you and others; you taste My joy and delight; you find rest and peace in My patient long-suffering; you trust and depend on My gentle kindness, goodness, and self-control. When you feast on spiritual fruit, I give you everything you need for any given situation you will face. All of Me for all that you face in your life."

"Eat until you are full, Mat'ta," Papa said.

I stood to my feet and removed a large cluster from the tree. The flavor of each orb was as varied as its color. The more I ate, the more I longed for God's presence; I wanted to know God, and be known by Him, holding nothing back. My heart and mind turned to adoration and worship. I closed my eyes, and hummed the words of worship I learned as a child. When I began singing aloud, the words I spoke were in a heavenly language, but I understood them in my mind in my own language. Lost in the communion, I remained in that position until I heard a loud thud.

Papa and Jesus erected the cross, the cross we carried up the Bridge, through the center of The Great Tree enclosed within the trunk and limbs of the tree. Simultaneously, streams of water began to flow from the base of the tree. Intuitively, I knew these streams were the life in the blood of Jesus poured out from His cross, but appropriated to my life as an expression of the eternal victory of Jesus. "The work of the cross has been done for you, Mat'ta. Now the work of the cross in you begins."

Chapter Ten

PREPARATION

Papa and Jesus ascended above the Great Tree, lifted high above ground. A beautiful crystal throne appeared and Papa took His rightful place, then He instructed Jesus to sit at His right hand. As I took in the beautiful vision of God on His throne, with His Son at His right hand, I discerned that the canopy of The Great Tree was also a throne. Seated upon that throne, as Shekinah Glory, was the Holy Spirit, as the reigning authority in the dwelling place of my spirit.

Holy Spirit proclaimed, "The chaos of your Innermost Being has been put in order. God sits on the throne. The walls of this kingdom are erect, and the breaches repaired. The enemies are evicted, and their plunder sits in the treasury of your God." A large treasure chest manifested under the canopy of the Great Tree as The Holy Spirit spoke. The chest held the gifts of inheritance. "Come close, and receive what we have prepared for you."

I followed His instructions and moved to open the chest. The item on top was a beautiful gown, made of fine, woven linen stitched with threads of gold. The beautiful brocade stitching formed the names of Jesus throughout the garment. I read the names slowly as I examined the beauty of the artistry by running my fingers over each name, "Advocate, Author and Perfecter of Faith, Beloved Son of God, Bread of Life, Bridegroom, Deliverer, Good Shepherd, Great High Priest, Light of the World, Lord of All, King of Kings, Messiah, Resurrection and Life, The Word." Holy Spirit said, "Step into the gown, Mat'ta. Be clothed in Jesus Christ. Put on his compassionate heart, kindness, humility, meekness, and patience." I stepped into the gown. It fit perfectly in every way. In my finite thinking, not taking into consideration the supernatural nature of the garment, I expected the gown to be burdensome because of the weight of gold within the brocade stitching. Instead, it was light and airy, and moved with ease. My memory filled my mind with visions of a day in my childhood; a beautiful summer morning, when I stood outside in the early morning sunrise, dressed in my mother's nightgown. I pretended to be a princess, a cherished daughter of a king, as I twirled the skirt of the nightgown. Joy and pleasure innate to abiding love filled my heart in that moment of my childhood; I could feel it all even now. It transcended this moment, as if the two moments were the same moment in time. I turned and twirled in circles to expand the flowing skirt of this garment. In response to my relived expression of pure joy, Papa spoke, "Mat'ta, you are the cherished daughter of a King. It is not pretend; it is fact." I twirled again, with my head back and my hands spread wide. In the mystery of God's supernatural power, the joy and pleasure that began in my childhood, transcending this moment, rooted itself deeply into my spirit. Joy was no longer an external emotion that comes occasionally; joy was an expression of my spiritual life. Clothed in the likeness of Jesus, my spirit was purely free, just as it had been as a very young child. "Thank you, Papa, it is magnificent! I had forgotten how life can be when I live simply in your pleasure."

"This is your Garment of Salvation, Mat'ta. I give it to you as a physical garment so that you can easily receive the supernatural truth of what it means to be clothed in Jesus Christ. The actual reality of being clothed in Jesus is much deeper; in time, that reality will expand within you. He continued, "In the days to come, you will need Jesus to be every name you read. As you come to know him more intimately, other names will appear in the stitching. You are always in Jesus, Mat'ta, not simply with Jesus." I twirled again, but as I came to a stop, the gown conformed to my body like a second skin. It was no longer a gown, but a part of my being.

"Because you are in your Garment of Salvation, it communicates your position as the royal daughter of the King. You are not an orphan and you will never be an orphan again. You are my child, my daughter, an heir." I looked again at my skin. To the common eye, the Garment of Salvation remained invisible; all I could see was my skin. However, when I rehearsed the names of Jesus and his attributes in praise, the gold stitching glowed and I could clearly see the Garment of Salvation. Visible or not, my identity in Christ is fact, and I am clothed in Him.

"There's more for you, Mat'ta." I returned to the treasure chest, and lifted out an ornate robe.

"This is your Robe of Righteousness. Examine it carefully. Take your time." I laid the robe out flat on the ground before me. Three words appeared in the design of the stitching: 'redeemed, justified, and free'; words written as a formal decree, a final verdict made as a judicial pronouncement in my favor. I traced my fingers over the three words. As I did, more words appeared beneath the final pronouncement. It was the legal evidence presented in my case: 'Holy Lamb of God Slain at the Foundation of the World'. "Papa, this robe is so regal and magnificent, I can feel your spiritual authority even as I touch the fabric," I said as I pulled the robe closer to my face to examine the intricate detail of the stitching. "Yes, Mat'ta, it is. It started out as the legal document Satan presented against you as evidence, and everything on it proved true. He had the rightful claims to you, until you cried out to Jesus to save and deliver you. Jesus became the decree, absorbed its hostility into His flesh, and washed it all away in His blood. Do you see the holes in the two corners of the robe?" He asked. "Yes, I see them." He responded, "Those are the punctures where the nails once secured it to the Cross. This hostile decree was Satan's strongest weapon used to rule over you, keeping you in slavery to sin and death. It was truth. The only way to remove it was to pay its penalty in full; and the only payment pure enough to do that was the Blood of the Lamb, slain before the Foundation of the World."

"Like your Garment of Salvation, we have prepared this Robe of Righteousness for you so that you can easily perceive the profound, eternal truth of what was accomplished for you. Pick up the Robe of Righteousness and twirl it above your head, Mat'ta." I did as Papa instructed; and when it spread out wide above me, it supernaturally attached itself at my shoulders. The puncture marks became the holes that looped around the beautiful jewels used to secure the robe in place. "Your sinful nature has been exchanged for Christ's righteousness. Righteousness is your identity, but it is also your covering and protection."

"You have been restored to the favor of Almighty God. Your past does not disqualify you for the work to which you have been called; instead, you are accepted in the righteousness of my Beloved Son, your Great High Priest." From the throne high above me, I could see Papa's expression of satisfied pleasure. I could not recall a time before this moment when I knew I had God's full approval. Papa is pleased, not just temporarily satisfied with my choices, but fully and utterly pleased.

Holy Spirit moved around me and in me at the same time. He captured the revelation 'God is fully and utterly pleased', and suspended time. "Mat'ta, seal this revelation by applying the blood of Jesus." Papa filled the treasure chest with light so bright I could not see anything within the light of His glory; in faith, I reached into the chest to retrieve what was suspended in the light of glory. I first grasped a chalice, followed by unleavened bread, and a flask of wine. Holy Spirit instructed, "Take communion with Me, Mat'ta. Together, we will remember what Christ Jesus has accomplished for you as the Lamb of God." I poured the wine from the flask into the chalice, and broke off a section of the unleavened bread. As I ate the bread and drank the wine, I thanked Jesus for all he is, and all he has done for me, until I came to the point of asking the Holy Spirit to apply the Blood to my life. I always picture myself dipping a hyssop branch in the blood of Jesus and applying it to the door of every opening of my being. "Loose the Blood of Jesus, with its resurrection power to this moment in your life." I did what Holy Spirit instructed with a simple prayer, "Blood of Jesus, be loosed. Pour over this moment of my life from the eternal moment when the shed blood of the Lamb poured out for me before the foundations of the world, until this moment. Blood of the Everlasting Covenant, be loosed; pour out the resurrection power, the same power that raised Jesus from the dead, into this very moment of revelation: God Almighty is fully and utterly pleased with me." I had never prayed this way before, but in this moment, I knew it was significant to do so. "Soak every breach in the timeline of my life. Fill up every chasm caused by sin. Make the path of my life straight again, removing the twisting and turning resembling the ways of the Serpent. Put my feet on the path of Righteousness. Walk closely with me, and guide me in the way I should go." As I finished communion a memory came to mind; the moment when I first believed I would never be acceptable to God because of my sin. Instantly I was back in time, as if it was present day, as I stood alone in my room, my sin before me, conviction weighing heavily on me, and shame filling my conscience so thoroughly I could not look at myself in the mirror before me. I confessed my sin, even though I have confessed this same sin in the past; but this time, I confessed it with my eyes open, looking in the mirror of that memory, "Please cleanse me of this sin, Papa. Loose the Blood of Jesus, with all its eternal, resurrection power to remove its corruption from the timeline of my destiny, and repair the breach so that I am back on track in the direction of your designs on my destiny. Soak the corruption of this sin in the Blood of Jesus, and absorb its corrosive effects in my life. Surgically remove it as if it is a cancerous growth; restore my health. Thank you, Papa, for the Blood of the Everlasting Covenant, shed before the foundation of the world, poured out from the precious Lamb of God." I knew this prayer was effective. I knew resurrection power instantly completed what I requested, and I was immensely grateful. I knew intuitively that Holy Spirit had just given me the most powerful weapon in all eternity: The Blood of Jesus. Knowledge concerning the Blood was powerful; wisdom for applying the blood was priceless. At the time of my confession of faith in Jesus, Papa removed my sin; however, this work of prayer was the restoration of His authority in me and over me. However long it took, I would walk with Jesus back into my past and apply the Blood of the Everlasting Covenant to every breach in the timeline of my life. At each breach, He will establish His authority, and I will receive restoration. For now, the work was complete. My mind was peaceful. My conscience was clear.

"Now, let me take a look at you, Mat'ta." As Holy Spirit swirled around me, His movement twirled me in the movements of a dance that pleased Him, dancing in the Spirit. My Garment of Salvation and Robe of Righteousness became visible and flew around me in waves of beauty. Papa and Jesus joined us, taking turns twirling me in this glorious spiritual dance. We laughed and sang in the Spirit until I was too winded to continue. Papa stepped in with a warm embrace. When He pulled back to look me in the eye, He smiled and turned me to face Jesus. Jesus declared with unmeasured delight as he moved in close to examine every slight detail. His delight and pleasure spilled out as laughter, and a declaration, "Mat'ta, it is glorious! You look exactly like me! You are a New Creation!" We all celebrated with shouts of joy, but I added squeals of delight. What a glorious day this has been! Just as we turned our last twirl of celebration the roar of a flood could be heard coming in off the ocean. We all turned in the direction of the sound. I stepped to the edge of the cliff of My Spiritual Life and leaned forward to focus in on the movement. It was not a flood made from waves; it was a flood of flames, and each flame was an enemy of God.

"When the enemy storms the shores of your Innermost Being, know that you are not alone. This is my covenant with you," says the Lord, "My Spirit which is upon you and in you; my words which I have put in your mouth shall not depart from your mouth, nor from the mouth of your offspring, from now and forever. You will pray. You will prophesy. You will declare the goodness of the Lord. And you will overcome the Enemy."

I held the Chalice of Wine and the Bread in each hand, raising both high above my head and declared, "The Blood of Jesus overcomes you!" Jesus, in His translucent, eternal body stepped over me, encompassed me, and stretched out his arms, as He had done on the Cross of Calvary, "No one takes my life from me; I lay it down willingly as a sacrifice for all humankind! It is finished!" Papa, in His translucent, eternal body stepped over Jesus, encompassed us both. Papa said as He drew His sword. It was no ordinary sword constructed of metal; it was a sword made of wood, the very Cross of Calvary. Papa raised it high above His head and drove the end of the cross into the cliff, and said, "Do not fear, Mat'ta. Nothing defeats the cross of Jesus. I have erected it at the center of your spirit. I can now apply all of its power and benefits for your victory. Stay focused. Take a stand, and remain firm in your faith."

Then Holy Spirit encompassed us all. He took the form of the Lion of Judah, large enough to fill the top surface of the cliff. Hidden with Jesus in God, I was safe under the cover of the Living Spirit of God. Holy Spirit roared. Not just any roar, but the roar of the Fear of the Lord. His power, might, and dominion met the oncoming flood of the enemy, pushed it back, and piled it high. The water rolled back from the shoreline and gathered as another tsunami wave, but this time it tumbled over the top of the impotent flood of fire sent from Satan, and instantly extinguished its threat. At the boundary on the shoreline, where the water once met land, stood the massive Wall of Papa's Kingdom. The Diamond Gate, reflective and bright in the Presence of the Living King, swung open wide.

Jesus leapt from the cliff's edge onto the tower of boulders that led to the shoreline. Papa followed close behind and yelled over His shoulder, "Welcome home, Mat'ta. Welcome home."

Connie Hartzler / Mat'ta

About the Author

I was raised in the Midwest. That sentence alone says a thousand things. Anyone who is also from the Midwest needs no more explanation. They get it; but for others, I'll explain. Family is everything; not just parents and siblings, but aunts, uncles, cousins, and grandparents. We did life together. Period. At twenty-two years old, I left Illinois and moved to Tucson, Arizona, where I reunited with my high school sweetheart, Gary. We married four years later. We both surrendered our lives to Jesus Christ in that four-year time frame, and built a life among a new family, our church. There's a saying, "Preach the gospel wherever you go, every day; when necessary, use words." That saying best describes our church family. We were raised up and discipled by many mature believers, who took us into their homes, into their hearts, and loved us like they gave birth to us. We did life together. Period. It was Koinonia fellowship.

Like so many other things, when true fellowship is simply part of one's everyday existence, it is easy to take it for granted or miss its significance and impact; but live without it, and it takes a lifetime to find it again. Living outside true fellowship became my Wilderness. Mat'ta is that story. Mat'ta is my story. Mat'ta might be your story.

The night God told me to begin writing, He promised me I

would be healed by the time the book was completed. So, in child-like faith, I typed Mat'ta as I experienced it. The prayer conversations with Papa really happened. I typed each visual description as I saw them, in the moment. When I got it wrong, or went off on my own tangent, my computer crashed, more than once, until I got the point that Papa wanted me to tell my story His way, not a story my way. Am I healed? Yes. The dark night of the soul has ended. I am no longer a prodigal.

I am presently writing the next book in the series, and I see that restoration is still coming, one conversation, one vision, one glorious day at a time.

conniehartzler@gmail.com

MAT'TA

By

Connie Hartzler

Connie Hartzler / Mat'ta

ISBN: 9781687207449

Amplified Bible (AMP)
Copyright © 2015 by The Lockman Foundation, La Habra, CA 90631. All rights reserved.

Made in the USA
Columbia, SC
02 September 2019